We'll Never Be Sixteen Again

By

Mick Whitehead

ISBN: 978-1-915889-55-3

This book is a work of fiction. Names, characters, places, organisations and incidents are either products of the author's imagination or used fictitiously. Any resemblance to actual events, places, organisations or persons alive or dead is entirely coincidental.

For Sue and Craig and all my family

Very special thank you to our editors
Paul and Chris

Book One of the Mark Byrne Trilogy

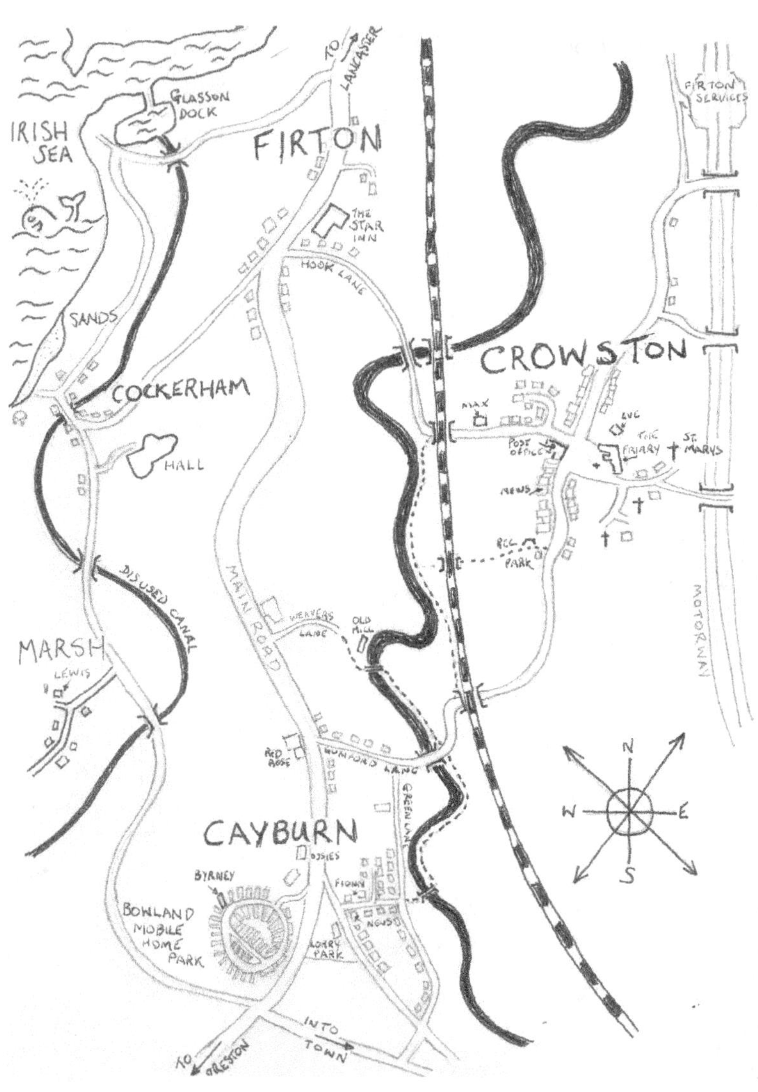

IRISH SEA
GLASSON DOCK
FIRTON
TO LANCASTER
FIRTON SERVICES
THE STAR INN
HOOK LANE
SANDS
COCKERHAM
CROWSTON
MAX
LVC
POST OFFICE
THE FRIARY
ST. MARYS
HALL
MEWS
REC PARK
DISUSED CANAL
MAIN ROAD
WEAVERS LANE
OLD MILL
MOTORWAY
MARSH
LEWIS
N
W E
S
RED ROSE
RUMFORD LANE
GREEN LANE
CAYBURN
BYRNEY
OSSIES
FIONN
NEWS
BOWLAND MOBILE HOME PARK
LORRY PARK
INTO TOWN
TO PRESTON

Chapter 1

Waiting On

Gratefully, I'm the only one stirring at 8.30am on a Saturday morning. I creep about in the kitchen doing my best not to make a sound, saves a lot of awkward questions when I'm trying to eat 'in a hurry' and especially when I'm nursing a bit of a thick head too. I reach up for the cupboard door and place my ritual, three Weetabix into a bowl, but as I bend down to grab the milk from the fridge, my Weetabix accidentally slide onto the Lino floor, bollocks! Picking them up and examining them, I take three new ones from the pack and position the dirty ones back from whence they came, our Anthony'll never notice. I crush the three bricks of wheat in the palms of my hands, shake the crumbs into the bowl and pour on plenty of milk. Spoon in one hand, bowl in the other, I make my way into the lounge and settle on the coffee coloured leather corner settee, looking out of our bay front window bathed in the early morning sunshine. There are no other stirrers about save a pot-bellied resident walking his pot-bellied dog. I follow the little furry piglet with my gaze to make sure it doesn't leave a deposit on our flags. My Fizzie (Yamaha FS1E Moped, my pride and joy) is parked at the front too. It wouldn't be the first time I'd found the aftermath of a cocked leg on my front tyre. Discarding my empty cereal bowl by the kitchen sink, I walk past my bedroom and open the bathroom door.

"Shit! Sorry Dad. Didn't know you were in here?" I step back and close the door. Oh that's not good, especially first thing in the morning! Dad is sat naked on the loo. I didn't hear him get up. Mind you he could have been there all night, wouldn't have been the first time he'd fallen asleep on the bog.

The voice from the bathroom is half angry with surprise "I thowt you'd gone!"

"Not yet, just need to grab my toothbrush" and as an afterthought "Please?"

"Well b' quick then!"

Head down, in and out, I grab my brush from on top of the sink; experience has taught me to hold my breath too. I quickly clean my teeth under the cold tap in the kitchen then grab my favourite red rally jacket. Feeling inside the pockets for my keys, I pull out a Robinson's beermat first instead, a souvenir from the previous night. Flipping the beermat over, examining both sides for any phone numbers, zilch! On departure I glance back at the kitchen: at the open cupboard doors, the dirty washing up, my crumbs on the floor; 'argh well, it'll have to stay like that'. I pull on my custom painted crash hat, down three steps in one and stride across the seat of my Moped; flip the side stand, rock the tank, *swish*, it sounds like enough to get me to work and back, key in the ignition, orange light aglow, kick start and off.

Visor up, over the resident friendly speed ramps, I like to think of them by their old name, sleeping policemen, more fun when you ride over them. Past the derelict hotel and the brick littered car park, visor down and up the Main Road, red lining the rev counter through each gear change to the screeching sound of the engine and the chill morning air, blasting loose the last, few, sleepy cobwebs. Red Rose Garage, turn right, down Gunford Lane, past Jayne Collins's Dad's mushroom farm, (she always kept me in the dark too), over the river, under the railway, leaning into every bend and accelerating away through thin, wispy white, shrouds of damp air, floating over me from the river. Coming into focus up ahead, the dark stone church steeples rise above the morning mist like exclamation marks 'Lording it' over us. Welcome to Crowston, three churches and no pub - hardly the wild side of life, but at least you feel safe. As I pull into a spare parking space next to Edward's car and dismount, I notice a couple of window cleaners on the opposite side of the square, stirring up the silence with their usual happy banter, takeaway coffee in one hand and their ladders slung over a shoulder. I get a momentary sense of captivity as I watch them wander off their next job and I'm about to lock myself away for a long, hard day's work. I always get the same feeling of confinement like my wheels are rusting whenever I gaze down from the motorway bridge and seeing all the cars below, hurrying off to horizons unknown.

The Friary café, integral VG store and attached domestic residence, with its faded Georgian grandeur, forms the eastern side of the small village square that is centred by a sad, splattered stone cross, unloved by all, save our feathered friends who bomb it with a familiar accuracy from the overhanging branches above. On the opposite side of the square lies, at one end, the rival corner shop and newsagent and at the other end, the Post Office then, crooked rows of patchwork cottages and car lined pavements, stretching out north, west and south. There is no market place these days. Gone an age ago too, are the lively travelling merchants and tinkers who would have wove, whittled and displayed their homespun handicrafts with pride and a tall tale or two. The old stone trough, filled by an unnoticed, underground trickle is possibly the last footnote to these forgotten times when the days passed by at a more gentle pace. Only a cobbled, borderless no man's land exists today for a few passing shoppers to idle over, as they habitually gather their daily bread, papers and gossip.

The personality of the village was having to grin and bear it, as it's inhabitants who were once upon a time mainly farmer types were now being rapidly replaced by the steady influx of the nouvelle riche from Lancaster, who were discovering village life in Crowston to be a stress free and affordable getaway from city offices. Quaint, three-storied weavers cottages were being spruced up and gigantic TV aerials sprang out from ridge tiles, where starlings had happily gathered since the halcyon days of horse-drawn hay carts.

The sound of happy whistling and rattling ladders grew distant and my yearnings temporarily subsided, I'd soon discover that, despite sacrificing half my weekend, hard work never killed anyone and the added perk for me was being the only boy in the company of young waitresses. Right then, I'd best get a move on.

**

I'd never actually given much time or thought to people's perceptions to the fact that I lived on a Mobile Home Park. After all, this was 1976, the high flying seventies, not a time for tarring the free spirited with the same brush, that we must all be a bad lot who inhabited colourful tin boxes on wheels. I mean come on; no one in their right mind would smear harmless souls like our elderly neighbours the Taylors in this way. The gentle Taylor's wouldn't say 'boo to a goose'. So when Madge was laying down the waggy finger in my direction, I was a bit put back to learn that my proud family home had a history of 'vagabond aspersions' attached to it in the shape of:

"If you ever take money out of our till, we'll know about it and you'll be marched off down to the Police Station."

Of course, I tried to hide my blushes by staring her out. I'd been working at the Friary for the last four months, mainly out of sight, out in the backyard, bailing cardboard, hauling crates of pop bottles into the shed, peeling potatoes, chipping potatoes and general dogs body type stuff; that was until 9.00am this morning. Madge looked into my young blue eyes and with her sergeant-major style bark announced,

"We're going to give you a go at waiting on in the café. You can have tables seven to twelve; Maxine will be along soon she has tables one to six; she'll show you what to do."

Madge's bark could strip the paint off a door, from twenty yards away. But at least you knew where you stood with her, preferably not too close. The Friary's popularity with weekend diners was fast turning it into a little gold mine. When Madge and Edward bought the café three years ago, aided by Madge's younger sister Joanie, it was nothing more than a run down, smoke filled greasy spoon that still had a spittoon mounted in the ladies toilets. They were both hard working Lancashire lasses who ran the business with military precision. Edward, by contrast, liked to chew the cud a little with the clients, but he pulled his weight in ways that either A) largely went unnoticed like taxi-ing everyone home at the end of a shift, or B) very noticeably being on the receiving end of one of Madge's explosions, for waltzing in from the other end of the café, when whole hell had broken loose in the kitchen and uttering something innocent to Madge like "How's it going my Sweet?"

But he did have real talent too, like how to bake scrumptious steak and kidney pies and prepare the base mix for the equally tasty sherry trifles. Ok, so perhaps Madge was right to have a go at him for stretching a simple two hour cash 'n carry run into a whole day, but that was Edward. You hardly noticed him when he was there but you always noticed him when he wasn't. Even Madge couldn't change him and for that alone you had to admire him. He saw himself as an old rooster, who fussed and clucked about after his two hens. When the three of them first began to make their mark here, some local villagers scoffed and made jealous remarks about how they were exploiting young kids as their labour force. But such people as these, that view life from behind twitching net curtains, were usually a mile off the truth.

The interior of the café had that fashionable 'mock Tudor' style, dark furnishings and a low ceiling that gave it an ecclesiastical feel. Its dark carpeted floor was swept every morning before opening time. Dark oak spindle back chairs and dark oak tables, with their solid old fashioned presence, complemented the wooden wattle framed walls that were covered in local prints and paintings from table height and upwards. Every conceivable space was given up to commercialism; nothing on display escaped a price tag. Shelves were decorated with books, jars of jam and pickles, perfumes, pot pourri and soaps. So here I was, clad in this shocking blue nylon smock jacket covering up my sex pistols t-shirt, thinking that the thought of nicking cash from the till had never even entered my head.

Every Saturday, regular as clockwork, the first customers through the bottom door were an elderly farmer type couple, known to Madge as Fatty and Thinny. They always arrived at 11.00am on the dot and limped and squeezed themselves into position at table ten. It looked to me like Thinny was catching up with Fatty in the waistband region. They ordered their usual, Homemade Steak and Kidney Pie and Chips, followed by Peach Melba for pudding. I was keeping an eye on them as their dishes had been scraped clean and were nearing departure. I had their bill made out ready and went to busy up in the kitchen for a few minutes. After emptying their dirty tray, I went back through to the café, to find their seats empty! I went through the café and down the three short steps to the gift shop and all the way to the entrance door, 'Christ, impossible as it sounds they must have done a runner on me.' What was I going to tell Madge? Not a good start; the till was down £7 already, balls!

Maxine came up to me a few moments later and held out her hand

"Here's your 50p tip." I looked at her blankly?

"Fatty and Thinny? (Gormless, meaning me). They always leave the same tip. I gave them their bill as I passed their table, OK?"

"Yes, fine, for a minute I thought they'd done a runner on me!" phew, what a relief.

Maxine laughed as she turned and headed back to the kitchen. I didn't know if I was pleased or angry with her, though come to think of it, Fatty and Thinny were hardly likely to run anywhere in their condition. I needed to relax a bit, not that there was any chance of that as the growing, steady stream of customers became a tidal flow by 4.00pm. I had no idea just how busy it got inside the café. As we rushed around, like blue arsed flies, I was starting to believe some of the village rumours about slavery and exploitation might be true after all; the good ship Friary was beginning to sink under its own weight of dirty trays, plates, tea-pots and soggy tea towels. It was all hands to the tables as the steam fizzed from the kitchen, mainly from the roaring deep fat fryers, but some too from Madge's pressure relief valves, either side of her neck.

My Friary shift every Saturday began at 9.00am sharp. It was the worse place to be on earth if you had a slight hangover - not that I should be hungover at sixteen years of age, but there was always an accommodating landlord, at some remote country pub, that would turn a blind eye to a small group of lads who turned up on their Mopeds. Two pints of Robinson's bitter was normally my limit and ensured I'd a ninety per cent chance of riding back home safely, without mis-timing a corner and impaling myself on a wooden fence.....usually. First job of the day, chairs on tables and sweep out the café carpet - gave us all a chance to say hello and talk about what we'd done the night before as our brooms scratched away the pattern. Somehow, the conversion never got around to asking Madge wouldn't it be more sensible to use a vacuum cleaner? (It would of course, but brooms are cheaper to run and besides our young muscles needed building up a bit).

Max began chatting "I saw this scary film at the pictures last night. Carrie – have you seen it?"

"No was it any good?"

"Well there was a lot of blood and the ending scared me half to death, everyone in the cinema screamed. The story line ended like there might be a sequel...a sort of a Carrie on. Sorry, that was an awful pun"

"No it was quite funny."

Maxine was three years older than me and just home from her first year at Bristol Uni. She'd straight, dark hair, cut into a 'Purdey' style bob, but her fringe was slightly skew-wif (a room mate at Uni had cut it). She had a thick set body, either that or the black café smock she wore was a size too small. She spoke eloquently, without any trace of a Lancashire accent, but what stopped me in my tracks was her broad smile, the way her lips flattened and thinned, pushing delicate creases into her cheeks, that made her hazel eyes light up and sparkle like jewels. Whenever we were in the same room together it was impossible for me to take my eyes off her.

Carpets done, we moved back into the kitchen. Vicky, a blond haired girl who'd been in my class at school was busy 'marjing up' loaves of sliced bread and repacking them. There was a knack to this and the first thing was not to tear open the bag. I found that out! Each pair of 'marjed up' slices were repacked face to face until the bag was full again. This saved valuable time later in the day. My next routine task was cleaning the café windows.

"Make sure you leave all the café windows open afterwards!" screamed Madge "otherwise, it'll be like a Dutch Oven in there today."

Yes, cleaning the café windows, I was made to use a wet dishcloth and some scrunched up old newspaper, no expense spared again. To make matters even more tedious, the café windows were tiny Georgian squares, with sun dried painted frames. Flakes of white paint gathered at the squeaky corners, together with bits of soggy newspaper. Like most jobs at the Friary it was a war of endurance over providence. With the windows now gleaming like port holes at sea, it was time to fill up a couple of buckets of chips. In the back yard (the only sanctuary from the endless orders) you could have a sneaky sit down away from the ever watchful Madge. Usually, you had to kick a path through a weeks' worth of discarded cardboard boxes, apparently left for me as I was the only one who bailed them up. Even rubbish had to be turned into cash. The bags of potatoes were peeled inside a rough lined drum that rubbed away the skins as it rotated. This was one of the few mechanical labour saving devices at the café. Once the skins were rubbed away the clean potatoes were placed under the chipper, one at a time. The potatoes were then held length ways over a square metal grid whilst you pulled down the handle, that pushed the potato through the grid and the chips fell into the bucket placed below. A bit like pulling the lever on a one-armed bandit and the winnings were chips, not shillings. Once two buckets had been filled and covered with cold water, they were taken through to the kitchen and placed next to the fryers. Next up, a bucket of whole potatoes cleanly peeled for roasting and boiling. (Don't forget to core out all the black eyes.) Madge thought I was rather good at this, handing me an apple corer. Little did she know I had an effort saving trick up my sleeve. I'd discovered if you left the potatoes running in the peeler long enough, the skins, black eyes and every little speck was removed for you. The trick was not to forget the potatoes were still going round and round as you did a bit of cardboard bailing. I did forget once and when I returned, discovered little snow white potatoes the size of peas. Madge would not have been impressed, twenty pence wasted at least.

Before the steady flow of customers began to roll up we were given a free lunch at 11.15am, a bit early but never look a gift horse in the mouth as my old Dad always says. We were given breaks for lunch and afternoon tea, which seemed to me to be an unusually generous act and Friary rules were, you could choose anything from the menu within reason. I say within reason, no one had actually said you couldn't have a T-bone steak but when word got around about Madge's Vesuvius style reaction when someone had asked for a simple slice of gammon, everyone stuck to the frugal safety of page one on the menu. So I usually followed Fatty and Thinny's example and plumped for the Steak and Kidney Pie, once tasted never forgotten and easy to see why we served so many of these tasty pastries in the café. We all lunched together, all six of us at the large table at the top of the steps. Conversation was usually minimal due to most of us being young, naïve and shy. Max who wasn't so shy cut in over the sound of the busy cutlery.

Max "You're looking a bit pale Byrney? " I hadn't heard half of what Max had said due to my head still being a bit wuzzy..

"Sorry Max, didn't hear you."

"I was just saying you look a bit pale."

"Yer, it could those two pints I had last night, been feeling rough all morning."

"Oh yes, where did you go underage drinking?"

"Moorcock at Bleasdale" I was trying to sound nonchalant like it was my usual Friday night.

"Any good?"

I remembered my blank beer mat "Yer it was okay, bit quiet for a Friday though. Sundays the best night when they have a DJ on."

"I might try it next time. It's been ages since I've been out there."

If only I had a bit more nerve, I'd ask her if she wanted to come along on Sunday. I could give her a lift on the back of the Fizzie. Not knowing Max that well, I thought she'd probably laugh if I asked her and besides, everyone else at the table was now listening too, it could be regrettably embarrassing. Just then, the bell rang on the entrance door down in the gift shop. The first new customers (not counting Fatty and Thinny) had arrived. Cue for us to clear our plates and get cracking.

Just a little over two weeks ago had been my last day at school. As it turned out, it felt like a real anti-climax. After all those years of schooling, the final few weeks kind of just petered out. Many had already left a month earlier at Easter break. The final day had been decreed a non-uniform day, whoopee! There were lots of photos taken in various odd little groups and gangs. Some walked around the playground holding hands; some took it upon themselves as a final chance to settle old scores, like Fionn who had longed to push teacher's pet and all round bossy boots Belinda Hunt into the school pond. That started a minor stampede as some of us threw themselves in, just for the hell of it. Belinda looked a proper mess, her coiffed hair do in ruins; her eye-liner running into her soggy clothes. She tried to put a brave face on it but Fionn had had the last laugh and many of us cheered and whispered to her, 'nice one Fi'. By 3.00pm we had all gone our sad separate ways knowing that most of us would never see one another again.

Four of us from Cayburn met up a few hours later, by the river bank at the bottom of Green Lane, but the river was too dry and shallow for swimming so we sat around talking and sharing a large bottle of Bulmer's cider. The summer sun was still hot late into the evening. None of us had any great plans for the future, despite this being our first evening of real freedom. My own plans to join the RAF had been put on hold until after my exam results were in and that was still several weeks away. We all had one thing in common and that was we all felt unprepared. Our teachers had concentrated so much on getting us through our exams, they had totally neglected to talk to us about what was really important in life, our future, job opportunities, money, what constituted a good and wholesome life; even how to chat up girls would have been more useful than reciting the table of elements. As the cider juices began to loosen our tongues, we all laughed about how the teachers had done nothing to mark our leaving. No prom do, no party, not even a slap up school lunch.

No doubt they all had a good knees up in the staff room celebrating the end of the class of '76. The only teacher who organised anything for us was our lovable Physics teacher Geoff Garrity. Geoff was probably the most likeable teacher in our school. He was a stocky shaped, middle aged guy with funny ad-libs - a kind of a boffin version of Les Dawson. When he'd found out about our uneventful farewell, he asked our class if anyone would be interested in a day out at The Lakes? If we all chipped in, he'd hire a minibus and pick us up outside school next Friday. It was a great, impromptu gesture; twelve of us had our hands raised before he'd finished talking. It was something to look forward to at least.

As the sky began to darken, the bats came out, swooping down above our heads and feeding by the river.Time for us to go. I walked Fionn home and we kissed each other goodnight, knowing we'd see one another again at work, over the remaining weeks of summer. As I walked the final steps back to the Mobile Home Park, I'd come to the conclusion I was going to save my money for a Moped tour. I reckoned three or four weeks would be long enough to get me on the road to....? Anywhere I fancied.

The afternoon in the Friary café was beginning to buzz, clatter and bang. The same was happening in the kitchen too. Madge was slamming two frozen T-bone steaks on the tiled floor to separate them. She was looking more startling than ever. It looked to me like someone had unkindly pulled down the skin on the back of her head as a baby and it had stuck like that ever since; her wild eyes and eyebrows were unnaturally high. I was giving her a wide berth before her eruptions started. It was normally Edward who lit her fuse with one of his tactless remarks, as he flounced into the roaring kitchen from his comfy chair in the gift shop to make himself another mug of tea. The steam from the deep fat fryers sizzled all the way up to the fluorescent lighting. Joanie had come down from the VG store to help out. She was doing her drying act, holding a dozen wet plates at a time and then filling pots of tea and hot water with urn tap permanently open. It was about then that someone noticed around thirty cyclists pull up and dismount in the village square. Madge asked Joanie to tell Edward he'd better open up the upstairs room.

"Byrney? You'll have to give your tables to Max and takeover upstairs, just give Joanie a shout if you need any help"

"You'd better look after these cyclists or you'll have Fionn to answer to, she's their favourite." Said Joanie only half joking and whose normally kind face was beginning to look a little more serious.

"Favourite? How do you know?"

"Last Christmas when Fionn fell off her horse and broke her arm, the cyclists all turned up here on Boxing Day with a Christmas present for her. When they found out she was laid up at home, they rode round to her house and delivered it to her by hand. So you'd better not keep them all waiting" she laughed.

If it wasn't busy before it was manic now. This is as bad as it gets on a Sunday and then there were around sixteen staff working and here we are, doing the same with less than half as many. I think Madge knew how hard we were having to work and eased up on her grumps. Even managed a joke or two,

"If you don't take these meals off me now, I'll come over there and give you a kiss!" That got your attention. The dirty trays that had been cleared from the tables lay all around the sink, on the kitchen floor too; they were in danger of lining themselves back up into the café. When the swing door between the café and the kitchen flew open, it was like treading through a mine-field.

Upstairs, the orders were mainly tea and toasted tea-cakes, so nothing too tasking until it came to making out the bill. A table of ten cyclists all wanted to pay individually and so on. Joanie appeared at the top of the stairs. It was so noisy, but from the gist of her comments and the expression on her face, she was both shocked and impressed by how many customers had made their way up here. Some, perhaps, had been hoping their bills would be way-laid under the deluge of comings and goings and others, who were still sat there, were squeezing the last dregs out of their tea bags. Max came up to give me a hand clearing up.

"My feet are so hot, she gasped, I'm going to have to take my shoes off, you don't mind?"

"No why should I? I replied laughing. They don't smell do they?"

"Do they?" said Max, looking aghast

"Only joking." And changing the subject quickly, "These cyclists don't tip very well."

"They're probably just disappointed because Fi's not here, nothing against you Byrney. We've done alright downstairs though. One guy was trying to chat me up, gave me two pound fifty"

"What did you do? Give him your phone number?"

"Certainly not! The old Spiv had terrible dental hygiene."

It was now or never, I thought. "Max, do you fancy a quick drink after we're finished up?" I could feel my heart pounding before the words had finished. Max looked at me. The question had taken her by surprise. "I need to go home first and have a shower but I'll be at The Star around 9.00pm if you're out that way tonight."

Bloody hell! Keep cool, don't act like an idiot. "Yer nice one, reckon we deserve a drink after the day we've had."

Joanie's kind face appeared again, with a stack of empty trays, as the last customers squeezed past us on their way out. There was a small landing area at the top of the stairs with a cupboard that normally kept all the spare clean cups and plates and also doubled up as a work station. The doors were open revealing empty shelves.

"Gosh you have had a rush on today, Joanie said, no one's realised you've had so many of them. I'll lend a hand to clear up too, we'll soon have it done."

One of the advantages of being part of a small team was when it came to divvying up the tips at the end of the day. Max liked to count the tips and stack them up neatly into six equal shares. £32.83 divvyed up equals £5.47 each - the odd penny was put back in the jar for luck. Nice little bonus, made all the hard work soon forgotten.

Mum and my brother, Anthony, were sat watching 'New Faces' on TV as I closed the front door behind me and dashed for a quick change. Inside my cubicle shaped caravan bedroom, there was just about enough standing space to open my wardrobe door and dress standing in front of it. Flares were out; drainpipes were in. I laced up my favourite blue Adidas trainers and combed my hair through with my fingers, head down, between my knees. Splash of Brut33. 'Yer splash it on all over Henry', I pictured my hero Barry Sheene and his gorgeous girlfriend Steph as they appeared in their famous TV advert, with Henry Cooper looking all bashful.

"I'm off out Mum."

Mum's eyes were still glued to the judges verdict on the telly "What already? You've only just come in, don't you want something to eat?"

"Nah thanks, already eaten at work" I noted Dads absence from the room "Where's Dad?"

Mum and I in unison, "Down the pub!" Mum looked away from the screen for a second and rolled her eyes as my brother Anthony stuck his fist into a bag of crisps and crammed them into his mouth.

"I'll see you later then."

"Don't be late back or you'll have your father to answer to," Mum said getting the last word in as usual.

Hopefully Dad would be unconscious on the sofa as usual too by the time I got back. Otherwise I'd be forced to listen to his same tired old stories. He always had an answer for everything when he'd had a drink, or if he hadn't, then he would refer to one of his drinking cronies who'd found a way to 'beat the system'. He won every family argument that way but he omitted to say that these so called friends of his ended up either in an early alcohol infused death or in hospital with cirrhosis. There was no reasoning with Dad in this state of drunkenness. Just suffer it in silence, until the words dried up and his woolly head slowly slumped to his shoulder.

The Star Inn at Firton was one of those new-fangled Beefeater Bistro's. Whenever I rode past up the Main Road, the car park was always full of flash cars: Jaguar's, MG's, Rovers and the like. Inside the decoration was flush and fussy; the pattern carpet even ran part way up the walls. Half the pub was given up for dining. The other half was quiet and comfy, the sort of place that made conversation easy and audible. It wasn't my kind of pub. I'd been here before only a couple of times after getting off at the bus-stop from Lancaster and cutting through to Crowston. There were only a handful of customers in the bar side of the pub and I soon spotted Max sat in the far corner, wearing a purple, suede frock coat. She caught my eyes as I made my way across, accidently kicking over an out of place bar stool which made her smile broadly.

"Hi" Max's eyes were heavily made up with mascara and gold coloured eye shadow; she looked even more appealing.

"You're just in time to buy me that drink. My first one didn't even touch the sides" she waved her empty pint Guinness glass at me. I placed my crash helmet on the chair next to her.

"Want another one of these?"

"Yes please," said Max teasingly. I walked across to the bar, blushing. I really didn't expect her to be here. I felt a bit nervous; she's out of my league; what was I thinking? I looked back at her as she lit up a cigarette. Not unusual, most of my friends smoked - cheap brands like Players No.6 or Sovereign. I noticed Max had the distinctive green and gold packet of St. Moritz Menthol.

Well, at least she'd taste nice if I was lucky enough to kiss her later. 'Behave yourself Byrney' I almost said out loud. After an awkward moment with the barman about how old I was and lying about how I was with my girlfriend sat over there in the corner, I returned to our table, successfully swerving to avoid the bar stool I'd kicked over earlier.

"So you're a Guinness drinker too?"

"Sometimes, makes a change" I said lying to avoid sounding like an amateur drinker. Not knowing what to expect I took my first sip.

"It won't bite you," said Max as she downed a good third of her pint in one go. I took a larger gulp, this time matching her mark. It was much more silkier tasting and smoother than I imagined. "You should try mixing it with cider, half and half. Gets you drunk quicker."

"Maybe next time, I'm driving, well riding."

"How do you like working at the Friary?"

"Well it keeps me off the streets, which keeps the pedestrians safe for another day. Actually I'm trying to put some money together for a trip I've got planned in a few weeks."

"Ooh sounds interesting, tell me more."

"Nothing much to tell, well actually I'd like to go on tour, maybe follow a few Bands around the country on my Moped for a few weeks."

"I noticed you were wearing a Sex Pistols t-shirt. You don't look like a punk rocker. Why haven't you got a safety pin through your cheek or somewhere?"

"I'm not that stupid. Corr imagine pushing a pin through your cheek. Knowing my luck I'd probably stick it through my tongue as well."

"I've a friend who has a stud in her tongue. She's having a party next weekend for her twenty first. We're all dressing up like punks in ripped clothes and stuff. Would you like to come with me? We're allowed to bring a guest each."

"Yer, why not! Where's it on at?"

"Her place, Cockerham Hall. Do you know it?" I'd been to Cockerham Village Hall once before, last November. It was my first Saturday night out on my Moped, nearly ended in disaster too. Coming back over one of the hump-back canal bridges, I'd narrowly avoided hitting a car. Somehow, I'd managed to swerve away at the last second in the glare of the cars headlights on main beam.

"Cockerham Village Hall, yer sure, what Time?"

"Not the village hall silly! Cockerham Hall, her Dad is Lord Nugent

"Are you sure?"

"Yes I think I know who Lord Nugent is," said Max looking puzzled.

"No I meant are you sure you want me to go with you?"

"Yes come along it'll be a laugh. You'll like Julie. She's really into 'double entendre'. Turns every word into a sexual connotation. The word 'it' (Max whispers) always refers to having sex. They're all stinking rich but they like to think they're very radical and with it." Just then, a tall, comical girl with carrot coloured hair and big teeth, smothered in 'over the top' lipstick, walked up to us and Max jumped to her feet and downed the rest of her pint.

"Byrney, this is my friend Julie, the one we've been talking about. Julie this is Byrney from work" Argh god yes I get it now, Cockerham Hall. I was being very slow on the uptake. I nodded at Julie and took a sip of my beer, trying not to stare at her big, red mouth.

Julie glanced down "And what's Max been telling you about me? Lots of naughty things I hope!" as she let out a hearty horsey cackle that I feared might loosen the windows. "Let's go Max before you turn into a cradle-snatcher"

"Sorry Byrney" said Max "Must dash, there's a nightclub waiting for us. See you next Saturday at work"

There go my romantic hopes, dashed again. Julie seemed mad as a hatter and a bit too well heeled for my taste. But, and there was always a but, Cockerham Hall? Now that does sound intriguing if not a little awe inspiring.

Chapter 2

Invasion

Wednesday morning, I'd an unexpected phone call from Joanie at the Friary. Two unexpected coach loads of tourists from Blackpool, out on a mystery tour, would be arriving in an hour; please could I come into work right away? I glanced down at my oily hands. I was just in the process of replacing my worn bike chain on my Moped so I'd need a lift. "We'll get Edward to pick you up" Blimey they must be desperate I thought. Gliding down Gunford Lane in Edward's brand new Ford Cortina Estate, Edward was pointing out places of significance.

"That's Collins's mushroom farm. He's my cousin. Did you know he went to Fulwood Grammar School and was in the same class as drummer Mick Fleetwood?"

I was impressed. I never realised Edward knew anything about pop music. Must be Madge's influence rubbing off on him. There was something slightly uncomfortable about listening to Madge sing along to the radio in the kitchen. Saturday before, she had sung along to Rod Stewarts 'Tonight's the Night'; it was hard get the picture out of my mind of Edwards black, stubbly chin and pie-belly smooching up to Madge looking all startled, *'...spread your wings and let me come inside...'*

Putting on my smock and stepping down into the kitchen, it was a great surprise to find Fionn at work that day too, having cycled in from Cayburn about half an hour earlier.

"So you've been roped in as well?"

Fionn "I don't mind, my day was cancelled anyway. I was supposed to be helping out at the stables but they were out servicing their stud." I'd no idea what that meant, so changing the subject,

"What sort of mood is Madge in today?"

"So far, so good"

The two coaches turned out to be mostly Scottish holiday makers, enjoying their annual fortnight in Blackpool. I'd never seen or heard such a loud rabble. The café was in chaos. Tables had been repositioned to accommodate larger groups and we were fast running out of Lager too. Edward was sent out on an emergency run to the Cash 'n Carry. That's the last we'll see of him today.

"Who's looking after the bottom shop?"

"Mrs Herbert. Fionn was laughing. Wait until you see her."

Mrs Herbert, as it turned out, lived directly next door to the Friary in a strange looking 'Hansel and Gretel' style wooden cottage that was almost completely hidden by overgrown Rhododendron bushes and Silver Birch trees. The only clue to there being a property behind the rambling woodland was a pair of green wrought iron gates that had been locked closed for an eternity, with a faded metal sign saying 'Private Property'.

"And she can speak fluent French."

The Jocks were getting louder. The café sounded like a battlefield. It was turning into a battle of wits too every time I took down an order. This involved much pointing at the menu, as their accents were so strong it was almost impossible to interpret what they were saying and the more they drank, the more their words just resembled strange noises. I was also getting worried that this could easily get out of hand; drunken Jocks had a reputation for running riot. The trick was to try and keep their faces stuffed with food and booze, so dirty plates were cleared away speedily and the next course arrived on the first return from the kitchen. On my first trip down to the gift shop to put order money in the till, I saw Mrs Herbert, standing behind the counter, smoking a cigarette through a long, bamboo cigarette holder. She looked like a character from an Agatha Christie novel. Her horn-rimmed spectacles were wonderfully old fashioned and she spoke with a gravelly voice. I'd never seen a face mapped with so many wrinkles and laughter lines. She was about seventy years old but looked a hundred.

"Don't mind me," said Mrs Herbert, as she stepped aside blowing a jet of smoke from the corner of her mouth. "I'm not meant to smoke but rules were made for breaking." I liked her instantly. She looked like she could tell a good story or two. She had moved over to the shelves and was turning all the labels on the jars around so that they all faced outwards. She seemed a bit doddery and fragile but her eyes were sharp to every moment. Living next door placed her in a very convenient position for helping out amongst all the shops in the village square. She had been a village resident since the end of the Second World War, beyond that her history was a mystery. Though there was a rumour she had been an interpreter in Churchill's War Office.

After a few hours, the Jocks were fully fed and watered and were finally getting ready to push off. One half drunken fella, in a Tam 'o Shanty hat, was having trouble opening his wallet, eventually parting with two Scottish ten pound notes,

"And have one yersen laddie" I took that to mean I could buy myself a drink. Normally I just take fifty pence out of the change and put it in the tips jar. Fionn was just passing the table when Jock number two grabs hold of her and sits her on his knee.

"You're a pretty wee lassie, how about geeing us a sang?" Jock two had no sooner raised his hand to commence conducting when out of nowhere Mrs Herbert had grabbed hold of Jock two's wrist and had a firm lock on it. I could see from the look on Jock two's face, he could feel Mrs Herbert did not intend of letting go until he released Fionn.

Jock, in the Tam 'o Shanty, spoke first, " Away Jamesie let the wee lassie go before Supergran snaps yer airem." Fionn sprang out of his lap and rushed off back to the kitchen. I followed her and met Edward, going the other way clapping his hands as loud as possible shouting

"Ladies and Gentlemen, your coaches are ready; please make your way out, thank you."

"Hark at him, trust Edward to reappear when all the work's been done. You Ok Fi?" but Fionn had a smile on her face.

"I don't know why I always seem to attract the nutters," replied Fionn, laughing at me. We'd been run ragged by this unruly rabble all afternoon so I decided, instead of putting change in the tip jar, I'd have a whiskey instead, and put the money in the till.

"What are you doing?" She'd caught me reaching up for the Bells Whiskey from the shelves in the cubby hole space between the café and the kitchen where the liquors and spirits was kept.

"One of the Jocks has just bought me a drink, so I'm having a whiskey. Would you like one too?" I said, winking at her.

"OK, why not? What the hell." I poured a small measure for us both and we both hurriedly knocked it back in one, spluttering as the sharp, fiery fluid hit the back of our throats. I put the bottle back in place quickly and we went on tidying up, each of us with a warm silly grin on our faces. At half past six, the Café was looking almost back to normal. I helped Edward unload the boxes from his car then he put Fionn's bicycle in the back and took us both home. As Fionn pushed her bicycle up her garden path I wound down the window and shouted, "See you Friday."

Fionn looked back over her shoulder "Friday?"

"The Lakes…our school trip!"

"Gosh yes! I'd forgotten all about it." Fionn's Mum came to the front door and waved at Edward's car as we U-turned and bunny-hopped around The Close on kangaroo juice.

"Still getting used to the gears," was Edwards excuse.

I received another phone call the following day asking me into work again, then Friday off and then back into work on Saturday morning as usual. At this rate it wouldn't be long before

I'd enough money for my trip. So far, I'd amassed forty-two pounds. I was aiming for a round figure of one hundred pounds for no particular reason other than it sounded about right.

Vicky was at her station in the kitchen, marjing up her loaves of sliced bread whilst Joanie was floating in and out of the kitchen in her normal cheery way and teasingly saying to me,

"Watch out Byrney you've got some competition."

Kevin 'the new lad' was out in the backyard with Edward, who was explaining the mechanics of the cardboard bailing machine. I just caught a glimpse of their conversation as I stuck my head around the back door to size up the new guy.

Edward had his hands on his hips and was giving out instructions, "Press the green button to start the compactor and make sure you keep your fingers well out of the way." I nodded at Kevin and stepped back inside the kitchen to find Madge had promoted me to stirring the gravy. A big vat of gravy was made up in the morning to see us through the whole day. The vat was resting across two gas jets.

"Keep stirring it," barked Madge "And whatever you do, don't let it boil."

When Madge had left, Vicky looked over, smiled at me and I said, "You can tell I'm her favourite, I get all the good jobs," not knowing if this was punishment or reward. I think Madge was a bit miffed because Max and myself had asked to leave at 7.00pm. Luckily Madge hadn't caught on to the fact we were going to the same do together, as otherwise she'd have no doubt burst into song, teasing us both with her current favourite, 'Save your kisses for me'. Not that it was strictly true 'we were leaving together' as I was making my own way to Cockerham Hall on my trusty Moped, with new chain, fully installed.

Cockerham Hall was perched about a mile north from the centre of the village and on a clear day you could see Blackpool Tower from the large, southerly facing drawing room. The gravel driveway was already littered with parked cars as I tottered slowly past them in first gear all the way from the Lodge house to the balustraded stairway. On the top step, stood a large, heavy pair of oak front doors. One was ajar. I was beginning to get cold feet. This wasn't my scene at all. The driveway was charmingly guarded on both sides by old fashioned gas lamps that had been converted to electricity and were now poised to warm up with a faint yellow glow. It was easy to imagine horse-drawn carriages being driven up to the grand stone stairway when the house would have been full of servants. I calculated there would be plenty of room for me to park my Moped closer to the hall as it too began to glow from the same sodium style ground floodlights. Everything about the house was large scale, but disappointingly very plain in style and lacked any finer carved detail. As I removed my helmet and locked it away inside my top box I could see silhouettes of guests inside the rooms. The music was cranked up full. I recognised the song immediately, 'Hey ho, let's go!'

I was wearing an old pair of black jeans that I'd ripped across the knees. My knees were nice and cool too having ridden the seven miles over from Cayburn. My plain white t-shirt, I'd decorated myself in black marker pen, writing 'Chaos' in large letters on the front and 'Filthy Punks' on the back with an added slashed scissor hole across my navel. I had some black eye-liner on too, that I'd borrowed off Mum's dressing table, but only applied it once I'd left home, in the reflection of my handlebar mirror - far from perfect; argh well, 'Hey ho, let's go!' I walked up the steps, in Dad's old knee length leather motorcycle racing boots. I stepped through the door into the large round entrance hall that vaulted through three floors, all the way to the globe-topped glass roof. The walls were covered with muskets and pikes. I turned around and was greeted by our hostess, the party girl, Julie.

"Who the hell are you? Don't worry I say that to all my guests. What do you think to my outfit, rude boy?" and she slowly pirouetted a full three-sixty. She had really got into the punk spirit, strapped up in her red bodice top with one pink breast exposed. I held out my hand and tried not to laugh. She bent forward and squawked,

"You're Max's friend aren't you? I think she's in the kitchen." I gave her a birthday card with a five pound WH Smith voucher inside as she slapped her ruby lipstick down my neck. I need a drink, quick.

"Where's the kitchen?"

"Through there, rude boy" pointing between two suits of medieval armour. I didn't hear her properly, but followed in the direction she had pointed. I looked around at the other rooms; they were all dimly lit and heavily populated, with sweaty bodies that stabbed about in the strobe lighting. The kitchen was like a bombsite, mainly due to the dry ice machine that had malfunctioned earlier and had filled the place with smoke. I saw Max talking to an old bloke with white hair and fake Dracula fangs that I later found out was Lord Nugent himself. How the other half let their hair down, I thought. Max spotted me and rushed forward plunging a can of cider in my hand.

"Fab you made it then. I wasn't sure if you were going come or not. Here, have this, you look as though you could use a drink."

"Thanks, I wasn't expecting it to be this wild. I can't hear a thing." I couldn't see much either, I said to myself. Max was wearing a pink wig that made her look more girly and definitely very cute.

"I like your make-up by the way; it suits you." I felt myself blush, but hopefully it went unnoticed, as I took a large swig of cider.

"Can we have a look around?" I made circles with my hand to help Max understand what I was saying.

"Follow me."

She grabbed my hand. I think she thought she'd loose me otherwise. We went through to what must be the large ballroom that was being used as a dancefloor. It was a mass of heads and limbs that were being illuminated by turning, overhead spot lights, Max's eyes lit up too, with excitement. Conversation was impossible. I suddenly got the urge to push Max in the direction of the dancefloor, which was vibrating to the rhythm of guest's pogoing up and down to the same beat. We'd no control over our bodies as our feet were lifted off the ground in the crush. It was like being in the middle of a cauldron of sticky, hot madness, but was stupidly exhilarating: More Ramones, more pogo-ing, more shouting along with the lyrics, '*Hey baby won't you take a chance, say that you'll let me have this dance and let's dance...*' From every direction, drinks were being thrown into the air continuously. Then we were straight into the next Ramones track, '*Hey little girl, I wanna be your boyfriend.*' The room was becoming smaller, as more guests piled onto the dancefloor. It was becoming harder to breath, so I caught Max's attention and pointed towards the exit. Just at that moment there was a sound of breaking glass, followed by screams and then laughter and the music scratched and slid to a halt. The record decks had been knocked over; time for some fresh air.

We found a large stone patio, just beyond a make shift fire door that had been wedged open by the DJ and we quickly left the mayhem behind us. Outside, the evening air, in fading darkness, was still radiating from a day of record temperatures. The weather had been stuck in a groove for several weeks now. We found a stone bench around the corner and sat down to catch our breath and to allow the air to find a gap under our clinging, wet clothes as the music started up again inside.

Max looked at me, "Was that your style of music?"

"Some of its OK, most of it sounds a bit babyish."

"But I've seen you wearing a Sex Pistols t-shirt?"

"Yer, I made it myself, just to get up my Mum and Dad's noses. They believe everything they read in the newspaper about the youth of today."

"So what do you believe in Byrney?" Max's question had caught me off balance.

"I don't know really, I'm waiting for it all to happen." I laughed but I could see from Max's serious expression she was waiting for a serious answer, so I paused, looked down to the ground then into her brown eyes and said, "I'd like to experience everything at least once in life."

"What everything?"

"Well you know, just to say yes to things instead of no"

"And how do you feel now that you've left school?" The truth was I didn't feel any different. I thought about my last day at school. What a let-down. Then, I remembered yesterday with Geoff Garrity in the Lake District. Everyone had been in a great mood. We'd sung a few funny rugby songs on the way up like 'There was an old woman of ninety-two'. We'd stopped for lunch at a roadside pub. A few of us had looked at each other about whether we should buy a pint or not. Geoff had said, 'you can have a drink if you want just don't ask me to buy it for you.' So one of us with the most bum fluff on his top lip (Mark Wilshire) went into the bar and came out with a tray of drinks. So, there I was, with a pint of beer in my hand. I looked across at Geoff who was wiping the froth from his top lip, grinning to himself and in that moment I was aware how something had changed. Geoff was no longer my physics teacher. He was now just some nice bloke who'd generously given up his day to give us a fond farewell. That warm afternoon seemed to float by. We ran up hills, playing silly games; then it was off to Bowness, for an ice cream ninety-nine and a row across the lake, two girls and two boys to a boat which ended in a water fight with the oars. Who needed a prom night and all that prestigious teenage angst? Not the last ones standing from the class of '76. Happy and exhausted we quietly watched the descending amber rays of the evening sun slowly disappear, on our journey home.

I looked up again at Max and began to waffle on, not feeling quite as convinced about life and yet it had been at that very moment sat having a drink with my teacher, that I'd realised I was stepping out into this mysterious world of opportunity and adventure and I was going to grab every chance that came my way. Something inside me was pushing me to see what was over the next horizon. Then something unexpected and immense occurred; Max put her fingers over my mouth to silence me and slowly kissed me full and long on my lips. I wasn't going to let her down so I kissed her straight back again for longer. I could see Max still had her eyes closed and when she opened them, I spoke with a satisfied smile "That was nice." All too soon our love bubble was burst abruptly by Julie's insane voice,

"Oh yes, and what are you two doing?" she was waving a finger from side to side. "Put her down Byrney you don't know where she's been."

Max grinned, "Very funny! Haven't you a party to see to?"

"Sorry Max, I need to borrow you for a minute. I'm having a spot of trouble with father. He's tipped up on the floor in the hall. I think he might be a tad pissed." Julie sounded more than half pissed herself.

"Right OK I'm coming." Max looked at me apologetically, shrugging her shoulders, "Back in a mo."

As they left, I heard the music crack up again, only it sounded more subdued than before. When Max returned, around thirty minutes later, wearing her suede jacket and minus the wig I knew the evening was over. "Sorry Byrney, we're taking Lord Nugent to hospital. His chauffeur is getting the car ready for him and Julie has asked me to go with her. She's just getting changed."

"What's happened?"

"He's obviously drunk something he shouldn't have. Julie thinks someone has spiked his drink, so we're going to get him checked over. Sorry I have to dash off like this. Would you like to meet up with me at The Star tomorrow night, say around eight?"

"Sure." We turned away from each other as an ambulance siren could be heard approaching through the village and becoming louder as it reached the driveway. Dizzy, blue, flashing lights whirled around; forming strange shadows against the hard masonry walls and Max disappeared into the mayhem. I watched as the back doors of the ambulance opened up revealing a clinical interior that looked like an empty refrigerator. A trolley was flipped into operation and carried up the stone steps. A crowd of inquisitive guests formed a guard of honour, as his Lordship was carried down and positioned into the back of the ambulance, Julie pushing a few onlookers aside who'd been impeding progress. I could see Max looking down and offering a few caring words to his Lordship, who was still wearing his Dracula make-up. No doubt the ambulance guys were relieved to discover it was only fake blood that his Lordship was wearing. I was still slightly bemused at his interpretation of punk being gothic horror. The ambulance departed in the direction of Lancaster Infirmary; that was the signal for everyone to leave. I walked back to my Moped feeling intensely sober, not so much through lack of booze but at that wonderful first kiss with Max. I felt three years older, I was catching up with Max at last. Life never felt so worry free and sweet. There was some unkind rejoicing amongst the drip of departing drunken guests, as I picked my way through the mass departure of slamming car doors and boot lids. *Punks One, Aristocrats Nil.*

Chapter 3

Meeting Eve

At home, we always ate breakfast at the kitchen table and when he'd not been drinking the night before, Dad was usually first to rise. There he was, clad in worn out slippers, grey slacks and a white vest, kissing Mum goodbye as he handed her the car keys. Mum was a manageress of a ladies fashion shop in Lancaster city centre. It was exactly ten miles away, but at this time of the day it would take her thirty minutes to arrive there.

"Eggs and bacon son?" my Dad enquired.

"Oo that'd be smashing, please." Dad was a dab hand in the kitchen. He fancied himself as a bit of a cook. Correction: he fancied himself no matter what. But, lately, he'd taken up the kitchen reins having less of a busy schedule than Mum. Dad only seemed to work when he needed money. He had a wagon parked up in the derelict hotel carpark at the entrance to our mobile home park. Hooked up to his wagon was a small trailer that carried a tarmac roller/vibrator. Summer should have been a busy time for him, but the heatwave was taking its toll on manual labour. Mainly due to the fact Dad's labour force was not very manly and would find any excuse to escape to the pub, which is where Dad usually ended up, to quench his raging thirst. So morning time was, happily for the rest of us, Dad's most coherent time of day and I enjoyed his company then. We were always on the same wavelength and could always see the funny side of life.

"No work today Dad?"

"Not really, just out prospecting. There are a few 'Sold' boards up round and about, so might chance my arm. Always a good time for new home owners to make a few improvements to their paths and driveways."

Dad would drive round in his little scouting van. He and another smooth talking 'know it all', Jim Calder, would tap up potential customers on the knocker. Once they'd landed a job, they were usually round at first light the following day, before the home owners had got cold feet. It was quite a profitable business. Tarmacadam cost next to nothing and, provided the ground didn't need too much prepping, most new driveways only took half a day to lay: one man on the rake, one man on the barrow and one on the roller. It was hot and smelly work, even on a cool day.

"What about you lad? What you up to today?"

"Working, two till six then might go out for a run on my Moped" Dad's face was wearing one of those what was I going to do with my life? expressions,

"Heard owt yet from RAF?"

"Still waiting."

Down in the bottom gift shop Mrs Herbert was standing in for Edward who'd had to pop out to Lancaster to get the ice cream maker repaired. Madge was spitting feathers at him earlier, for letting it breakdown when we'd sold out of ice cream the day before. That'll be him gone for the rest of the afternoon then. Mrs Herbert smiled at me as I said hello and rang my first order into the till and counted out the change. Standing aside, she was puffing on a filter-less cigarette that she had removed from a fancy blue packet. I'm attracted to its unfamiliar design and picked it up to take a closer look.

"Git aines"

"Gitarn," Mrs Herbert corrected me. "Its French for gypsy." Her voice sounded croakier and as she spoke her wrinkles radiated in all directions across her fine, leathery face, her eyes keen as mustard behind her 'Catwoman' spectacles. She let out a sudden cough and waved me and the cigarette smoke away.

Half an hour later, I was back down in the gift shop. Mrs Herbert was sat down behind the counter, with her eyes closed, looking slightly distressed.

"Are you ok Mrs Herbert?"

"Not really. I'm having a bit of an attack of coughing" and she coughed uncontrollably hoarsely to prove her point. In the news, old people seemed to be dropping like flies in the current heatwave but in Mrs Herbert's case it was probably her Gypsies.

"Do you want me to fetch Joanie?"

"Yes that would be wise, I think you'd better" she spoke with shallow breath. The shop bell rang and I followed two new customers up to the tables and left them to choose a seat, whilst I go through the kitchen and up into the VG shop to find Joanie.

"It's Mrs Herbert. I don't think she's feeling so well."

Joanie sighed, "Oh not again. Let's have a look at her." I followed Joanie's quick stride, back down to the still silence of the gift shop. Joanie peered at Mrs Herbert who was now looking like death warmed up, but at least her coughing has subsided.

"Byrney, take Mrs Herbert next door and stay with her. I'll phone the surgery to get someone out to her. Give me your orders, I'll take over your tables for a while."

Right so I'd got to look after this old lady, blimey this was a new one. I was not feeling very sympathetic at being totally out of my comfort zone. We walked out of the gift shop door and round the dividing wall. I wasn't exactly holding onto Mrs Herbert, as she seemed to be doddering along under her own steam okay. I was sort of stooping beside her and walking in a Groucho Marx type way, with one arm in front of her and one behind, in case she fell one way or the other. It must have looked very comical to anyone watching. After only a few yards, we turned right and into the wild unknown that was her front garden. A few more steps further and the village was lost behind the overgrown bushes, then the pathway wheeled around to the left to reveal a strange looking wooden bungalow that was like something straight out of a fairy tale. There were plant pots of every shape and size underneath the two shuttered windows, either side of the porched, front doorway. The house was painted leaf green and the door and window frames a lighter shade of green with cream coloured edges. By the side of the door, a small, frayed French flag looked oddly out of place and was hanging in the still air. Mrs Herbert removed a bunch of keys from her apron and unlocked the three Yale locks. I helped her with the top one. The door was pulled open by a giant metal door knocker, in the shape of a gloved hand holding a small cannon ball. Mrs Herbert led me inside. The rooms were much brighter than I expected, lots of gilt framed mirrors and ornate furniture. Mrs Herbert slowly bent down and stretched one leg over her chaise lounge. Short of breath, she managed to whisper a few words.

"Please get me a glass of water Byrney, there's a darling," as she bent down to remove a small brown bottle of tablets from her handbag that was tucked in at the side of her seat. I returned from the next room with a glass from the sink that I'd rinsed and half filled with water. Mrs Herbert smiled, took the glass and winked at me and whispered,

"Half measures eh what?" I watched her swallow a few pills and empty the glass in one.

"Shall I get you some more Mrs Herbert?"

"No thank you, don't make a fuss, I'll be right as rain in a minute or two, it'll pass," Her voice was recovering slightly. I glanced around the room at what appeared to be the contents of a well-stocked small museum. On her mantelpiece was a bronze bust of a young child with his gaze fixed up at the ceiling; it was next to half a dozen photographs, framed in odd shapes and sizes. I checked Mrs Herbert again and she was looking much less distressed; her eyes were now closed and her horn rimmed glasses were hanging across her neck, still attached to a silver lace. In the kitsch surroundings of the Friary gift shop she had looked old and uncomfortable. Her eyes gave her away like it was something that she had to endure. But here in her home, amongst her treasures and stretched out on her chaise lounge like a canvas masterpiece, even with her present pains, she was quietly glamourous. I crept over to her fireplace to get a closer look of her framed photos. I started from the left. The first photo was of a middle age couple, in some tropical place by the sea. A man wearing white baggy trousers and white shoes had his arm around his partner. They both looked happy and were contently smiling. Maybe the woman was Mrs Herbert when she was younger? The next was a studio photo of the head and shoulders of the same man looking younger and was signed in the bottom right hand corner *'Je t'adore mon cheri, Paul '* A real smooth operator, I thought, in his dickie bow tie. Then came two photos of groups of people gathered together wearing dinner jackets and a smaller photo of an older couple who I presumed were the Smoothy's parents, as the father had the same receding hairline, but even more exaggerated. They were stood on the steps of a large hotel entrance, but the name was partly obscured by the branches of a palm tree. Lastly, the largest frame was of a young woman in army uniform, probably from the last war. I picked up the frame and could just decipher the name above the breast pocket ' Lt. Larouchamps'

"That was me, thirty-five years ago." I turned round in surprise as Mrs Herbert was now sat upright and wearing her specs again. I rested the photograph back down in its place on the mantel. "Were you in the army Mrs Herbert?"

"Yes but I wasn't very useful. And please don't keep calling me Mrs Herbert, its Eve."

"Okay Eve, did you work for Churchill by any chance? Some of the girls at the Friary think you were once an interpreter for the War Office."

Eve pointed across the room with her crooked, bony finger "Go, open the top right hand drawer of my bureau." I walked across to the bureau that was sideways on to the large bay window, where most of the sunlight flooded through and bathed the whole room in a warm, golden light. The lid rested open and there were several small drawers inside. I noticed the shadow from the open lid formed a diagonal line down the front of the bureau and the sunlight had bleached the part that was exposed. It had obviously rested in exactly the same position for decades. I grabbed the small wooden knob and the drawer flew out, almost spilling the contents. Inside were old diaries and a small blue box.

"Yes bring that over to me please." I passed her the small, blue cardboard box and she flipped open the lid. Inside, lying on white coloured silk, was a medal with a green and red ribbon. The medal was in the shape of a cross with a pair of cross swords. "This is what the French Government gave me after the war. But I don't think I deserved it really. There were a lot more people, ordinary people, much braver than I ever was."

"What happened?" I said quietly, not hiding the fact I was hugely impressed. I could see she was more energised as she held onto her medal box and that she was eager to talk about it. As she began to speak about her experiences, I looked around the room again. Lots of nice ceramic jugs, vases and plates, all decorated with painted flowers; the room had an easy, cosy feel to it. I could feel myself sinking deeper into her richly upholstered, high backed fireside chair. It was so homely and somehow inspiring to see a lifetime of relics and souvenirs.

"It began about six years before the war. I met my husband to be in Paris, so romantic. We married and moved to Nice to run the family hotel. It was a family business that his grandfather had started at the end of the last century. It wasn't very grand, but Paul my husband knew a lot of musicians and artists, even a few second rate film stars and there were many parties in those carefree days." Eve drifted into her memories for a moment.

"And then in the summer of 1940 shortly after the fall of France, my world was turned upside down." Eve lit one of her Gypsies and pulled hard on the bamboo holder. Her forehead frowned as she took in the strong, stale smelling tobacco . I noticed the ends of her fingers were stained with nicotine too. Then, through her thin dark lips, she blew out the thick, pale smoke towards the ceiling.

"Then of course the parties were no more. It became impossible to carry on living that way, under a regime of hatred and reprisals." Then suddenly, bringing me back to the present, there was a knock at the front door and a familiar, friendly voice called out,

"Mrs Herbert? Byrney?"

"We're in here." I answered and Max's bob-tailed head appeared round the door.

"So this is where you're hiding, time's up Byrney! Joanie wants you back in the café. She's asked me to sit with Mrs Herbert until the doctor gets here."

"Oh don't make such a fuss. Sit down for a minute both of you. It's not often I have young visitors." Eve began to cough again with excitement and she laid back on the chaise lounge in defeat. I took her cigarette from her and left it to run out in the ashtray on the copper topped coffee table, that separated our two seats. Max was perched on my chair arm. I stood up and Max slid into the unoccupied seat as we swapped places

" I'll get her another glass of water" I said, raising my eyebrows at Max. "Eve's been telling me about when she used to live in France before the war."

"I never knew you lived abroad Eve, how lovely" said Max sounding similarly impressed.

"You'd be surprised at the things I've done and shocked too. Maybe I'll tell you about it someday, but not right now. I think I'll rest my eyes again for a few moments."

"I'll get going Eve. Hope you're feeling better again soon." Max followed me to the front door.

"That was a nice surprise seeing you come in just now" I said to Max smiling. She put her arms around my neck and half teasing said "How nice?" I was beginning to catch up to her.

"This nice" I said and gave her my best kiss.

"I think you'd better get going lover boy," was her cool response. "I'll let you know about Eve when the doctors been." Reluctantly I let go of her, realising I'd taken long enough in returning to my afternoons work.

Back inside the café Joanie was explaining to me how Mrs Herbert had lived alone in the village for the last twenty five years. "I don't even think she has any relatives either, certainly no children. She never speaks about the past. Like most people I know who'd fought in the war, they want to forget about it and move on" I thought well, maybe now's the time Eve wants to tell someone about it and for some reason that person was me. Joanie finished up by saying "I'm sure she'll be fine. Don't be fooled by her frail looks, she has fire running through her veins that one."

Later that evening I got a call from Max.

"It's another girl for you," said Mum, making me blush in my unawares.

"Who is it?"

"She says her name is Max" Blimey, this was a bolt out of the blue. I'd not given Max my phone number, as I was trying to keep her a secret, until I was more confident about how long we'd be going out together. Mum rolled her eyes, as only Mums can do and handed me the phone. I stretched the coiled cable to its full extension so that I could close the door between the lounge and the kitchen. Privacy was almost impossible in our mobile home, which added to my embarrassment about sharing my private calls with all and sundry.

"Hi Max, how did you get my number?" I was trying not to whisper too quietly.

Max completely ignoring my pathetic question "I'm fine thanks. Just thought I'd let you know what the doctor said about Mrs Herbert. I could tell you're fond of her. I didn't realise I had competition," she joked.

"Yer right! What did he say? Is she going to be okay?"

"Yes, he did some blood tests and told her to rest, but she looked completely fine by the time he left."

"That's good!"

"Are you doing anything right now? Would you like to come over?" said Max calmly. I suddenly felt nervous with excitement.

"Yer sure! What number do you live at?"

"Twenty-four, how soon can you get here?"

"About twenty minutes, might have to buy some fuel on the way."

"Perfect" and I heard her blow me a kiss down the phone and then hung up. I put the phone back down onto its receiver in the lounge and dashed back into the kitchen, before the inevitable, motherly interrogation. "Who's Max?" I ignored her question as I closed the bathroom door. Quick brush of my teeth, head down between my knees and run my fingers through my hair, a waste of time as by the time I'd worn my crash hat, my hair would be flat as a fart. Slipping on my jacket and leaving my bedroom I could see Mum stood blocking the door to the porch, arms folded, looking a little more serious.

"Who's Max?"

"Just a girl at work. I'm just popping back up to Crowston for an hour, I'll be back soon"

"Don't forget your door key and no drinking!" She kissed me on top of my head, as I slipped past her.

"Don't wait up, Love." I said imitating Dad's voice.

"Don't be cheeky." Last word to Mum.

There was only a faint swish of petrol as I rocked the fuel tank. Need to buy some then. I stopped at Cayburn Garage, as the locks wear about to be clammed onto the pumps for the night. The garage forecourt had a black, thin, rubber tube running across it and whenever a wheel ran over it, a bell rang inside the attendant's kiosk. My mate Lewis likes resting his front wheel on the tube just for devilment, until Ozzie's exasperated, red face appears at the hatched window, cursing and swearing. No need to ring the bell tonight.

"You know how to time it!" said Ozzie wearing his usual oil stained white overalls.

"Sorry, can you squeeze in a gallon and some two-stroke oil please?"

"What ratio?" grumbled Ozzie

"Twenty to One." This was one of the few garages along the Main Road that had a two-stroke oil dispenser. I should carry some spare just in case but I always forget to buy it and besides I don't have time. Ozzie wants to lock up and I've got a hot chick waiting. (Hopefully, no one can read my mind)

I was counting the numbers down Hook Lane, trying to keep my bike straight at the same time, twenty, twenty-two then a long gap to a break in the hawthorn hedge and two low brick walls, arcing up to a pair of brown, wooden gates that had been pushed open to just more than a car's width. The detached house was painted white, with a gravel driveway that had grass growing up the centre. At least my old man hadn't been here recently, spreading his tarmac. I flipped my bike onto it's stand and pressed the doorbell. I could hear music playing inside and then it suddenly got louder and a voice shouted from above.

"What do you want?" I stepped back and looked up to see Max leaning out of the window. "Come on up, the door's open." I opened the glass panelled door and immediately noticed a huge crystal chandelier, hanging in the hallway, that almost touched the floor. I saw Max's shoes, lying as though they had been thrown off in a hurry, beneath the dark wooden coat stand, so I slipped out of my trainers with the laces still tied. Apart from the music drifting down the wrought iron staircase, the house sounded empty. I climbed the wide stairs two at a time, pulling myself up on the shiny wooden handrail. The cream carpet looked new and immaculately clean, as did the rest of the house as far as I could see. There was a yellow and black hazard sign, attached to what I guessed must be Max's door that made me smile. Quick pause to check myself, I was still holding my lid (crash helmet). I opened the door to find Max sat on her bed, leaning against her pillow, her bare legs bent at the knee and her feet tucked in close.

"Hi" I said waving with my free hand.

"It's Okay, come in, put your helmet down" She smiled. "Who's this?" she said, referring to the music, as I walked over and sat at the end of the bed. The next track had just begun and the intro sounded like an orchestra on the front row of a starting grid.

"No idea, Beethoven?" Max laughed and passed me the Album cover. On the front, was a collage photo of a large, gloomy, tenement style building. I stared at it until I noticed that some of the windows had been blanked out and individual letters printed – 'Physical Graffiti'.

"The track you're listening to is called Kashmir? Led Zeppelin?" I was trying not to look any dumber than I felt. "Where have you been hiding? We played this all the time at Uni last year. Just close your eyes, listen, feel the movement the instruments make and see where it takes you." I closed my eyes and pictured Max's smile. The music was hypnotic. "Just let yourself go," whispered Max. I listened to the lyrics about a distant land and I began to imagine horses being driven, with soldiers on their backs, escorting an ancient Queen, moving fast towards a safe haven.

"Well, what do think?"

I was too shy to admit what I thought, so instead said "Maybe a bit spooky. Think I need to listen to it a few times first." I was trying not to sound like it was a cop-out. "What do you see?"

"I see mourners, beside a funeral pyre, like they have in India when they send their loved ones down The Ganges on a burning raft, or even better, a Viking, floating out to sea on a burning ship, surrounded by weapons and gifts on their way to Valhalla." She laughed "Really gets to you eh? When I die, this is how I'd like to leave this world. Sorry I'm boring you aren't I. Go ahead, you chose a record." I sat down on the carpet by the bottom shelf of her bookcase and thumbed through her album collection until I saw something I recognised and then, with instant delight, pulled out Steve Miller's 'Fly Like An Eagle'.

"I've just bought this last week; I love it, do you mind?" I was about to lift the needle off the Led Zep album when Max moved forward and flicked a lever.

"Press the Eject"

"Thanks," I said, feeling all fingers and thumbs. I gently rested the album on the turntable, side one, track one, 'Space Intro'. "I got hooked on this, listening to the radio in Madge's kitchen, to the 'Paul Gambaccini American Top One Hundred Show' every Saturday afternoon." The music faded to a distant beat of a monitor as the sound of air rushing over a wing lead into the opening riffs of track two, 'Fly Like An Eagle'. "Where do you buy your records Max?"

"Ear 'Ere in Lancaster. It's just a market stall, but they have a really large selection if you like Prog Rock; not much Punk, but they do import from America too." She had climbed back into the hollow on her bed.

"Next time I'm in Lancaster, I'll check it out. My Mum works there. She's the manageress in a clothes shop called Jade, do you know it?" I was hoping that dropping the fact my Mum was a manageress might impress a little.

"No, I don't think so"

"What does your Mum do?"

"She's an interior designer but its mainly boring stuff really, like wallpaper and curtains. She works away quite a lot, in Stately Homes."

"Is that how she knows Lord Nugent?"

"Kind of, they were at Cambridge together too. He always had a crush on my Mum."

I studied Max's book shelves. As well as rows of paperback novels, there was a pile of old Jackie comics, a lava lamp and at the end sat a child's doll that looked oddly out of place. It intrigued me and was about to pick it up when Max said, "Please don't touch that. Come over here and sit down."

Max's bare legs were beginning to get under my skin. I felt conscious that I was staring at them too much but I'd the feeling that is exactly what I was supposed to do. I took a chance and rested my hand on her knee, but Max lifted it away, followed by another one of her enticing smiles. I wondered if Max could see my eyes light up.

"Just listen to the music." Time really was slipping into the future. When the track had finished I said "Do you ever think about your future?" Just lately it had felt like it had become an obsession with me: my exam results, joining the RAF perhaps, Mum and Dad saying 'get a job'; me, staring at cars driving up and down the motorway. Where were they all going? And here I am, just a fleeting glimpse in all those lives?

Max "No not at all! I only believe in the here and now."

"What about all your friends at Uni and stuff?"

"They're not here now are they!" she replied. I never thought about it in that way before. I was always either looking back, or rushing to see what was on the other side of the next hill, what was round the next bend. Perhaps I'm missing out on what's really happening now. Feeling the barmy outside temperature warming up the room I suggested we take a walk, "The river must be quite close?"

"Great idea! Let's go." Max picked up a check shirt and threw it over her shoulder, shaking her hair into shape. At the foot of the stairs, Max stepped into her sandals, pulling the straps around her ankles and holding onto my arm, to keep herself from over balancing. I was beginning to feel overdressed for the hot weather, in my trainers and ripped jeans - the same ones I'd worn at the Punk Party. That was the trouble with riding a Moped; you always had to cover up as much skin as possible. I locked my helmet inside my top box and we sloped off, down Hook Lane, in the direction of Five Arches Caravan Site.

When we reached the low stone railway bridge we turned left into a narrow field of tall grass with a well-worn path cut through, leading to a gap in the dry, hawthorn hedge. Just beyond the gap, the riverbank cut in closely, making the pathway just wide enough for one. I let Max lead the way, for no other reason than I could secretly watch the hypnotic movement of her limbs. The air was noticeably cooler. There were hoards of midges and crane flies hovering lazily over the still, shimmering, shallow water. Max looked round and confessed, "This is my favourite walk. We can carry on and bend around the village and come out by the old tennis courts if you like?" Her words filtered through the evening birdsong. I could see why she liked it here; it felt so intoxicating.

"Did you play down here when you were younger?" I cringed at my own words; they sounded really naff.

"Yes all the time, I used to pretend I was a princess in an enchanted world," I didn't know if she was being serious or just taking the piss.

"I meant don't you have any brothers or sisters?"

"No, just me and Mum" I was going to ask her about her Dad but there was something in the way her words were cut short, that gave a certain finality to them, like a doorway being bricked up. In the short space of time I'd gotten to know Max, she rarely spoke about her family. The pathway lead away from the river and along the edge of a parched field of wheat, with hanging heads of seeds. The bare path was so dry it had fissures and cracks the size of the San Andreas Fault. I was racking my brains thinking of something to say.

"What do you think to Eve - Mrs Herbert?"

"I like her a lot too. She has charisma"

I was keen to hear more about her adventures. I always had a deep, protective respect for elderly people ever since I was a small child. I remember one harvest festival at Infant School; a boy and a girl were selected to help deliver the school collection of fruit and vegetables to the local home for the blind. That Autumn, I was the boy who was chosen by the headmistress. We sat in the back of the headmistress's car, holding onto our baskets of fruit. As the large, menacing mansion house grew closer it was impossible to see beyond the long heavy curtains that were drawn behind all the windows. I was expecting all the people inside to be asleep in the dark, stuck there with nothing to do. But when I met them, I was really impressed by how lively and quickly their minds worked. They were chatty and actively involved in playing games, like cards and dominoes and despite their unimaginable handicap that they lived with from day to day, they seemed all the more supremely intelligent. From then on, I always said to myself, 'never under estimate old people'. Eve struck me as a person who knew every trick in the book, to coin one of Dad's phrases. Max was right too; she did have charisma.

"Did she tell you anything about the old days, before the war, when she was married to a French guy?" I said, striding out to catch up with Max.

"Yes, can you picture her? She used to slouch across the lid of a grand piano and sing whilst her husband played. She reminds me of Bette Davies. I saw her recently being interviewed on Parkinson and she was really frosty towards him"

"What do you expect?" I laughed, "He's from Yorkshire!" We reached the deserted tennis courts and next to them was a small recreation park with swings and a merry-go-round. I can never resist an empty swing.

"Come on!" I said "Last one to the swings is a Cissy." Max tripped me up and got there first.

"Cheat!" I shouted after her, in a cloud of dust. Max won the race to see how high we could get on the swings too. I was feeling like my man-hood was taking a beating. We wrapped the swings around the frame and went to sit on the grass, which was now starting to feel damp, with evening dew. The sun had slipped out of the sky. I turned onto my side to face Max who was chewing a stalk of grass and trying hard not to look at me.

"Did anyone ever tell you, you had a fantastic smile?"

"Sure all the time."

"No, seriously. It really knocks me out."

"I hope you're not going all sloppy on me?"

"Nah, I can resist you any day of the week." I joked.

"What, even this?" and Max pressed her lips against mine. We lay there side by side pointing out the first stars, for what seemed like an eternity. I was still thinking there was something just waiting around the corner to get me. But I brushed these apprehensive thoughts away and said to myself, 'just the here and now'.

I don't remember much about the walk back to Max's house, just the sight of the brand spanking, blue MG sports car, parked on the drive with the hood down.

"Mums back! I'd better go in." She dropped my hand and ran to the door. I just had time to squeeze in a 'See you Saturday' as Max waved the back of her hand at me above her head, as she disappeared inside closing the door quietly behind her. I strapped up my helmet, closed the lid on my top box and wheeled my bike out of the drive. What a beautiful night! I was beginning to learn more about Max and the more I learnt, the more I felt I was losing myself inside her.

Chapter 4

Laugh! I Nearly Cried

Another Saturday here again, already! My mates all said I was mad when I took this job at the Friary. Waiting on tables! Like it was supposedly an unmanly thing to do. That was only part of it and besides; it was so busy I didn't have time to worry about whether it was damaging my street cred. Unmanly or not, no one laughs at you when you have a fistful of one pound notes in your wallet. I grabbed my blue smock from the washroom, as usual at the start of the day and walked towards the kitchen to hear Madge hollering for me to go and see Edward, who was waiting for me in the backyard.

"You're in for a treat this morning." Did she sound mysterious or threatening? You could never tell with Madge. Edward greeted me with his usual gaze, over the top of his spectacles.

"Morning Byrney, it looks like a bomb-site round here. Can you get some of this cardboard shifted before the others get here?" By shifted, he meant 'bail it up Byrney'.

"Okay Edward." He could see the disappointment on my face. I thought I'd moved on from this job.

"Don't worry, we'll soon have it cleared." '*We*' I thought, as Edward disappeared back into the kitchen. As I was compacting down the last of the cardboard, these old farmer types began to appear, walking through the backyard and up into the rear garden, where the big wooden shed stood, which housed all the bottles of soft drinks.

"Grand day for it Ned!" said one of the cloth-capped farmers sucking on an empty pipe. It took me a minute to realise he was talking to Edward (Edward - Ned, oh I get it). Then a couple more appeared, sleeves rolled up, braced and belted. 'Blimey!' I thought 'It's the Wurzels!' I could tell they were all relatives of Edwards, as they were all wearing the same dark brown, Cordy-Roy Pants. Now I was beginning to understand what Madge had meant by, 'I was in for a treat'.

"Is this the one Ned?" said the Wurzel with the pipe, walking round the back of the shed and scratching his chin. I had still no idea what was happening, until one of the other Wurzels opened the shed door, looked back at Edward in amazement and spoke in a slightly irritated way, "Well tha'll have t'get this lot shifted before we start!" Edward knew full well the shed was still full of crates of pop and soft drinks.

"Yes, don't worry; I've got it all under control. Byrney 'ere is going to take all the crates out. I'll get us all a mug of tea organised." Cheers Ned! So it's just me again then?

"Come on Byrney! Don't dither about. Just take all the crates over to the back wall and stack them up there for the time being." The crates, stacked three high, made very comfy seats for the Wurzels to perch on and start chin-wagging to one another. I'd just about finished, when Edward reappeared, with a tray full of steaming mugs of tea. I was looking at the last few crates of pop and was wondering how long they'd sat in the back of the shed. The labels were badly faded, covered in cobwebs and the liquid inside had separated leaving a thick, coloured ring around the neck of the bottle. Nothing was thrown away. Once the shed was fully emptied and the mugs of tea were drained and all the reminiscences of sheep stories had died away, Edward stood up and said,

"Well Gents! What do you reckon?"

The plan was to move the big shed closer to the top step and turn it around, so that the door was closest to the step. I'd no idea why. Later, I found out that they were having a new, walk in freezer delivered in two days' time. The Wurzels began walking round the shed, stretching their braces. Some were inside testing the strength of the wooden floor, by banging it with their boot heels.

"How about, if we all grab hold of the front end and lift it up, whilst someone slides a roller under it, then all's we have to do is push it along?"

"Aye, that should do it!" they all agreed. Now we're getting somewhere at last, I thought. But the ground was too uneven for the rollers to roll.

"Well we'll just have t'carry bugger then!" The Wurzels all spat on their hands and rubbed them together. If you can't beat 'em, join 'em, so I did the same. No sooner had we lifted it again than there was an almighty, ugly, splitting sound, as the shed roof collapsed and the four sides folded out like a house of cards. When t'Wurzels had picked themselves up off the grass and the chuckling had subsided, Wurzel with the pipe said

"Well Ned, should be a lot easier to move now!" And that was that. The shed was reassembled later in the week and luckily, by the following Saturday, all the crates were reinstated, in their newly located position.

"Have you done it?" enquired Madge, when I returned to the kitchen looking worse for wear.

"I'll let Edward tell you" I said, as I dashed out to change my smock. I could hear Madge scolding Edward and he promising to have it all done in time.

"Don't worry my Sweet, it won't hold up installing the new freezer."

It was a slow afternoon in the café. Madge was eying the clock and wondering where all the customers were. Then someone mentioned the men's singles final at Wimbledon was taking place.

"Well I wish they'd bloody hurry up and finish it!" Madge roared. Borg eventually won it, 9-7, in the third set against the foul-mouthed Romanian Ilya Nastase who was employing every dirty trick in the book to upset Borg's cool. At 4.30pm, the trickle of customers was returning to near normal level. There were just enough of them to justify opening up the top floor, so these extra tables were shared between me and Fionn. Fionn was was covering for Max as she had swapped her usual Saturday for a Sunday, because her Mum was taking Max to the Theatre in Manchester and the upstairs cyclists were happy to have their favourite waitress serving them. I could hear them calling her name, out of fake desperation, like they were calling for a nurse.

"It's so embarrassing" complained Fionn although I could tell she was enjoying all the attention. After a tidy up, Madge called us to go, one at a time, usually starting with the person who had worked the longest or hardest. It was her way of letting the skivers know she was on to them, by making them wait until they were last to leave. However there were no shirkers on a Saturday, unlike a Sunday when there was a huge gaggle of waitresses and Madge couldn't possibly keep track of them all. The tips were much lower today thanks to the Tennis.

I raced home on my Moped as I'd arranged to meet up in town with Lewis. Mum dropped me off at the bus stop. Lewis was already waiting, in his leather jacket and spotted shirt, which was open wide at the neck, with a long collar, on the outside of the open jacket.

"Have you put your apron away for the weekend?" was Lewis's greeting. I chose to ignore that one. We caught the Preston bus and jumped off outside the Roebuck Inn at Bilsborrow. The pub was fairly quiet, apart from a couple of drunken navvies, playing pool. We ordered a couple of pints and went and sat down near the pool table. There was no change on the side of the green cloth so Lewis put a ten pence piece down, to wait for the next turn. The navvies paused in their game and eyed us up with an ominous intent. Navvy one, with black face and stubbly chin, decided to take exception to us.

"What you staring at kid?" I assumed he was talking to me, as Lewis was sat opposite me, with his back to them. I didn't know what to say. I judged by his aggressive stance that I would be damned either way. His playing partner broke the deadlock,

"Come on Owen, finish the game." Aggressive navvy decided to play on and then, as he was lining up his shot, he stood up straight again and pointed a finger at me,

"I'll bend your fuckin' nose the other way for you, if you don't stop staring!" I got up and moved into the other bar and Lewis followed. The two navvies finished their game, slammed their cues down on the table and disappeared out of the door, pocketing Lewis's ten pence in the process.

"What the hell was that all about?" I said to Lewis, who was half smiling and sighing with relief. He hadn't realised they'd nicked his ten pence.

"We could have took them on, easy."

"Oh aye? You didn't say a right lot when they were threatening us"

"Just a pair of pissed up navvies," said Lewis, smiling like he knew what he was talking about, "Let's have another pint." Part way through our second pint, the pub was filling up with middle aged couples who looked respectful enough to us and the atmosphere in the pub became more relaxed and cheery. We downed the last dregs and counted the rings of froth that circled the inside of our glasses, six each. "Come on Byrney it should be getting a bit lively now, might be some spare going."

We walked up to Bilsborrow Village Hall and handed our tickets to the doorman. The Bilsborrow Saturday night disco wasn't one of our usual haunts, but as Lewis had been given a couple of free tickets from a mate who was doing the DJ-ing, we'd nothing to lose. Typically it was a non-alcohol bar in the village hall, but Lewis had a small bottle of vodka, hidden in his inside jacket pocket, that we shared with our cans of coke. The disco lighting was a bit lame, two sets of traffic lights that actually looked like they'd be back on the road come Monday. The seating was set out along either side of the hall and was occupied by under-age girls, who got up in groups and danced around their handbags. I was feeling a bit out of place; it was a good thing Lewis had brought the Vodka. Occasionally, a girl would approach Lewis and say, "will you go out with my mate?"

"Which one's your mate?"

"Over there in the black boots. She really fancies you."

"What's her name?"

"Liz"

"Well tell Liz to go and grow some tits!" After about half an hour of this, we decided to head back into town and catch last orders at The Shepherds.

Outside the pub door we recognised a few of the Mopeds parked up and we reached the noisy bar just in time for Andy Dunne's round at the bar.

"Where you two been all ponced up?" growled Andy

"Bilsborrow!" replied Lewis and sensing the usual following on question from Andy, said, " Don't ask! Byrney almost had a fight with a head case in the Roebuck."

"Yer, some drunken lunatic didn't like the shape of my nose." I chipped in.

"You should have chinned him Byrney lad," suggested Andy, "get in there first with a head butt."

Thanks guys! I was trying to put that unsavoury episode to the back of my mind. It was easy for him to say. Andy never stood for any sort of nonsense. No one messed with Andy. He had the sort of permanent expression that made you automatically check where the nearest exit was, in case he took a shine to you. He looked much older too for his age, having a five o'clock shadow and sideburns that met up somewhere under his chin. He was dating a girl called Tracey, who was about a year younger and therefore under the age of sexual consent. She was a pretty little thing and a precious, pretty little thing in her father's eyes too, despite Andy making it obvious to all that he'd had every inch of her. He also delighted in rubbing salt into Tracey's father's wounds by groping her at every opportunity, in front of him.

Andy handed each of us a fresh pint "Fill yer boots lads!"

"Cheers Andy, where's Tracey tonight?" I enquired feeling obliged to have a quick chat with him.

"Its Saturday night Byrney lad. Never bring yer bird out on a Saturday, besides she's on t'blob."

"Romantically put." Wish I'd not said that quite so loud as I noticed Andy's expression go flat.

"Eh? Come again?"

"I was just saying, you've got her right where you want her"

"Too true Byrney lad" and his expression took on its usual smugness again.

Phew! Got away with that one. Poor Tracey, I thought, having a big lump like him on top of her. But on a good day, when no one was looking, Andy could be a gentle, caring bloke. According to Lewis, who'd been to Andy's house a few times, said, he always looked after his Mum and saw that she had everything she needed. Andy had never known his father. He used to joke to us that he was just a lorry driver, on an overnight stop, who'd filled his Mum's head with fancy talk and empty promises. Without a father, Andy had no one to peg him back and consequently he did whatever he wanted. His Mum tried her best and that was good enough for Andy, 'She's a diamond' he'd say.

Next morning, Sunday, I wake up with a thumping headache, looked at my bedside digital clock, 10.05. I could hear Mum and Dad in the garden, talking in a mumbling, inaudible way. I sneaked a peek at them from behind the corner of my bedroom curtain. They were sat on their aluminium framed sun loungers, getting settled in for a day in the bright sunshine. Dad was reading the newspaper and Mum was drying her nail varnish, her hands open wide and stretched over the edges of the plastic arm rests. How did they manage to look so comfortable on those horrid looking things? When they eventually got out of them, you could see strap marks on the back of their legs, where they had rested against the plastic webbing. I made myself a brew and went gingerly back to my bedroom to read a book, which Max had recommended: 'The Eagle Has Landed' by Jack Higgins. It was a well written war story that was having an infectious effect on me, to the extent that I was thinking of reading it through in one sitting.

When I was half way through reading it, sat in the lounge, I suddenly thought I should give Max a call. Everybody was still outside in the garden, pretending they were somewhere else like the Costa Brava. Ironically, the temperature here in West Lancashire was hotter than Lloret-de-Mar, ninety degrees Fahrenheit. Dad had a plastic cool box next to him and had filled it with bottles of San Miguel Beer. He was busy explaining to Mum how they were saving money not having to fly to Spain this year. I could tell Mum wasn't convinced. She liked to get away; mostly from Dad. They all seemed pretty well occupied, safe for me to pick up the phone. The dialling tone rang and rang. I was just about to put down the receiver, when Max picked up.

"Hi Max it's me!"

"Yes"

"How's things?" I could tell there was something wrong; the pauses in between were hanging, like a judges sentence.

"Had a bust up with Mum again yesterday and I didn't go with her to Manchester."

"How come?" I was feeling uneasy about the answer, maybe she was about to dump me.

"Usual stuff, the latest is she's always telling me what to wear, how to do my hair and make-up. I'd just had enough and she stormed off to her boyfriend's house, I guess."

"You've been on your own all day?"

"Obviously."

"Do you want me to come over?"

"No I'm okay, just need to sort a few things out in my room. I'm back at the Friary tomorrow, to make up for taking today off, so just having a quiet day." Well, at least I don't have to worry about Max having found someone else.

"I've been reading that book you told me about, 'The Eagle Has Landed'."

"Yes do you like it?"

"Yer, I can't seem to put it down."

"Glad you're enjoying it. I really like the Liam character. He reminds me of you on his motorcycle."

"Must be my Irish eyes," I said laughing.

"Yes, and your cheek. Thanks for cheering me up. I finish at 4.00pm tomorrow, maybe you can meet me outside?"

"Love too" I sounded a little too enthusiastic.

"Bye Byrney." and she hung up before I could say good-bye.

Max's version of growing up without a father was very different to the way Andy had handled it. For one thing, she never spoke affectionately about either of her parents. Max's Mum was career minded who fussed and fashioned over her designs and tastes. It obviously rubbed Max up the wrong way, but there was something more between them. I sensed a vulnerability about Max too, that day in her bedroom. There was something that Max was protecting herself from.

I was reading long into the night. I'd challenged myself to finish the book in one day and so I had to prove I could do it. It was 2.00am and I still had a chapter left to read, when I heard a rustling outside my bedroom window, followed by Mum and Dad's bedroom light being switched on and Mum saying "There was someone walking around outside, I can hear their footsteps on the gravel at the back." Dad appeared in the passage way. I turned my light out, as he passed by. I could hear something too and turned around in bed, to reach for my bedroom window. I eased it open slowly and there in our garden were two fat badgers, waddling past. I slipped back down into bed and listened to Dads footsteps, as he circle around outside.

"There's no one about, you must have dreamt it," whispered Dad, sliding their bedroom door closed, as he slid back into bed.

"Well I'm telling you, I definitely heard someone moving about John."

"Well there's no bugger out there now!" said Dad audibly loud.

"Shush, you'll wake everyone up," said Mum audibly louder. Then their bedroom light was switched off and peace returned. The war story I was reading fizzled out too. As it turned out, it was all for nothing. The only guy to get away was Liam, on his motorcycle.

Chapter 5

Eve's Story

I wasn't sure about going in to the Friary on my day off, so I waited outside. In the downstairs lounge of Madge and Edward's house, I could see Fionn and Kevin having their afternoon tea. When working, we had to use their lounge in the afternoon for meals, as there was normally no free space available in the café. Fionn saw me and waved so I took off my helmet and waved back. I'd brought Anthony's crash helmet with me in case Max wanted to go for a spin on my bike. I was the only one amongst my mates who'd passed their Moped Driving Test. Lewis had took his test a week earlier than me and had failed on the walking pace manoeuvre. It almost caught me out too, but I just managed to wobble through without putting my foot down in the road. It was a great feeling ripping up my L Plates. To me it was like a badge of honour, only minus the badge. Just then the front door opened and instead of Max it was Kevin and Fionn standing there asking what I was doing? Giving me a couple of whoohoo looks and whistles when I said I was waiting for Max. Kevin said "A few of us are going straight to The Star after, if you fancy a pint?" I'd promised my Mum I wouldn't drink while out riding but one or two wouldn't hurt.

"I'll see what Max says"

Kevin, "You under her thumb then?" I could feel myself blushing then Max came out of the shop door below so I ran down to meet her. I could hear Kevin and Fionn laughing in the distance behind me.

"Hey up!" as I caught up with Max.

Max "Let's pop in and see Mrs Herbert."

"You mean Eve?"

Max smiled "Yes, let's pop in and see Eve then." I wanted to put my arm around her shoulder as we walked along, but was conscious of people from the Friary watching us as we walked past. The garden side gate was slightly ajar, so we took that as a good sign, that Eve had been out and about recently. It was strange how after only a few short strides, all the noise and hustle and bustle of Crowston filtered away to near silence. It was like stepping into another world. Maybe it was another world, if any of Eve's stories were to be believed.

"Look at you two, Max and Byrney. Entrée, come in." Eve was looking very cheerful and a little glammed up holding a round cut glass goblet, with a cherry balanced across the rim on a stick.

"Cocktail hour!" she said, "What can I get you?"

"Nothing for me thanks Eve"

"Oh come along Byrney, I'll bet you've never had a Singapore Gin Sling?"

"Yes, come on Byrney" said Max mockingly.

"Ermm.." after a few moments' hesitation and Max reminding me about how I wanted to try everything in life at least once, I agreed to have one, if Max would too. Eve had one of those globe tables, where the lid opens up to reveal half a dozen bottles of spirits and an ice bucket with the word 'Ricard' across it. She was no amateur barman. Ice, gin and another four unknown ingredients all disappeared inside her silver cocktail shaker. I could have sworn she cracked an egg into it too, but I must have been seeing things. As she shook up the mysterious potion, she looked at the two of us, raising her thin eye brows and winking secretly to Max in a moment of fun.

"This will put hairs on your chest!" Eve proclaimed delightfully and she emptied the contents into three, pink glasses. I bent forward and raised the glass to my lips, whilst they both waited for my reaction. Nothing to it I thought, as the cool, smooth liquid slid down and then the kick hit you, at the end, right between the eyes.

"Wow!"

Eve was pursing her lips "Not too strong I hope?" Max took a gulp from her glass and breezed straight into conversation,

"Are you feeling better again Eve?"

"Yes fine, darling. I've been given one of these to help me breath." And hiding behind her armchair was a small oxygen cylinder on wheels, with a mask attached to it via a clear plastic tube. Eve insisted we both had a go on it too. The effects of breathing pure oxygen and drinking sing-along-a-gin things were beginning to make me feel giddy.

"Have you got any more stories Eve?"

"You mean my escapades from the war?" I could see Max relaxing back into her chair. She looked like she was nestling down for the duration and it wasn't just the drink; it was the featherbed surroundings of Eve's lounge. "There should be an old photograph album in the bureau, second drawer down, we can start by looking at those." Great, I thought. I just love looking at the history to be found in old black and white photographs. I handed Eve the black and gold bound album with a gold sash cord hanging loose that was used to mark her page. She opened the album and rested her arm across the first page and looked at the sun shining through the window and said,

"I suppose it all began down in Preston just after the First World War.

Father was an industrialist who owned and ran a foundry in Preston making ships propellers. He lost everything, in 1932 during 'The Great Slump'. He suffered from delusions of grandeur and always wanted the best for me, his only daughter. When I was sixteen, he sent me off to finishing school at Luzern in Switzerland. There, at an old chateau by the side of Lake Geneva, I was taught to be charming and how to acquire a husband. They also taught me to speak French fluently, but I had other plans. My father never understood my ambitions to be an artist. So with what little savings I had left - I was no debutante, unlike the other girls whom all had Earls or Viscounts for fathers - I packed a bag and caught a train, alone, to Paris. It was still far enough away to prevent my father from sending someone out to bring me back home again.

I was able to find a few, temporary assignments, doing translation work for a book publisher and in my spare time I went along to Madame B's evening art classes, in a tiny garret in Montparnasse. My new friends were all very artistic and knew other artists, poets and composers. In the late 1920's, it was the best place to be in the world, so vibrant, so exotic; the things I saw in 'The Revues' there would have been inconceivable at that time in Great Britain. Then I met my husband to be, Paul Larouchamps. He was in love with Cole Porter, not the man you understand, but his music and his liberated lyrics. None of us wanted to feel the same constraints that straight-jacketed our parent's generation. We were married at the Registrar Generale, with only our close friends in attendance and afterwards we celebrated at the famous Brasserie Lipp on the Boulevard Saint Germain. The day after our wedding, I received word from our family solicitor that my father had taken his own life; there was barely enough money left from the sale of his factory to clear his debts. He'd known where I been staying in France all along, but pride had prevented him from letting me know that he faced financial ruin. Soon afterwards we moved to Nice, to help run Paul's family hotel business. When Paul's father passed away, too soon afterwards, we breathed new life into the old hotel. Many of our old friends dropped by and came to stay from Paris. Paul knew such a lot of show people, singers and dancers and silent movie stars like Marcel Vidert and his beautiful wife Helene Tarly. You must have heard of them? They were very big in France" Eve rose up and automatically filled the cocktail shaker again and refilled our glasses as she continued to talk.

Max picked up her legs onto her seat cushion and smiled amorously at me. "I'm not boring you both, am I darlings?"

"No Eve!" Max and I said together.

"Please carry on," I said hugging my glass.

"Our hotel was a big success and we were able to buy an apartment in the Lympia quarter, down by the picturesque, historic port. We had a fantastic life. Then when France fell in June 1940, to begin with life became so overcrowded. There were thousands of people flocking to Nice, people of all nationalities. The city became one of the few gateways out of France. Guests were coming and going all the time and when the resistance groups began to operate, we were asked if we could look after Jews and others in our cellar. There didn't seem much danger in it as we had the perfect cover but, later, when we were hiding airmen who'd been shot down over France, we had no idea what we were getting into. Our organisation had grown so fast and involved too many people. We were always very careful but, looking back on it now, I can see we took enormous risks: breaking curfews, delivering messages by hand and harbouring soldiers for days, sometimes weeks at a time.

After a year, there was very little food available and we were buying everything on the black market, through our contacts in the resistance. Then eventually, the inevitable happened and when some of our friends were betrayed, Paul insisted that I leave immediately. He bought me a ticket and I sailed to Gibraltar, Paul promising he would meet me there in a few days, once he had found safe lodgings for his mother and younger brother. I went down to the dockside every morning, to meet the new arrivals as they embarked, but Paul wasn't amongst them. My money had all but run out and the only way back to England was free passage aboard a hospital ship, if I volunteered to help with the wounded soldiers from North Africa. Those poor boys, I wanted to save them all." Eve lit up another of her Gypsies and started to cough. I passed her the oxygen mask but she refused to take it, "You have it!" She continued with her story and flipped through her photograph album pausing every once in a while to point out a man who had died fighting or some other act of bravery.

"When we docked in Southampton, I continued working and nursing for the sick and helping to repatriate Algerian refugees. I sent letters to Paul's mother in Nice every week. I was desperate to find out what had happened to him, or if he was even still alive. I worked long hours at the military hospital; it was the only way to put my fears to the back of my mind. Then, exactly two weeks before VE day, I received a letter from France, confirming what I'd known in my mind for a long time, that Paul was dead. Paul had intended to join me within a week of my departure, but all the ports along the south coast where being closely watched and guarded, day and night. The only chance to get away was to take the guided escape routes over the Pyrenees and into Spain. But there were many dangers, as collaborators had infiltrated some of the guide organisations. One morning, when his group were sleeping in a barn after an overnight trek, they were woken by the sound of approaching motorcycles. The occupants were soon rounded up. The guides and the farmer were arrested and taken away to be tortured at the nearest Gestapo headquarters. The rest of the group were locked inside the barn, whilst the German soldiers set fire to it. Those who tried to escape were shot and killed, Paul was one of them." I was expecting Eve to become emotional, but her eyes were defiant. Joanie was right about Eve, she does have fire running through her veins.

"When the war was over, I moved back to Preston. There was nothing I could do to change the past, so I said good-bye to Eve Larouchamps and became Eve Herbert once more. It had been over twenty years since I'd last been in Lancashire and very few people remained whom I knew. I found cheap lodgings by the docks and took a job on the ferry boats that ran from Preston in those days to Northern Ireland. It was not pleasant work. There were always lots of drunken men fighting. Then in 1955, out of the blue, I received a letter from an old friend in Nice; it was Pauls younger brother Henri. He had spent a lot of time trying to track me down. The only address he had for me was my father's old place in Kirkham. I wrote back thanking him for his letter and to my surprise, a month later, Henri arrived in England. When I met Henri it was quite a shock, he looked so much like Paul. He brought with him an old suitcase with some of my old personal possessions, like my treasured photograph album. There were lots of tears but like I said, it was all in the past. It was obvious Henri also had visions of a romantic nature towards me, but he just wasn't my type. Then he said that he had brought some money for me, which had been lying in a bank account in Nice that had belonged to Paul and he gave me a cheque for twenty thousand pounds. I couldn't conceive it after all this time. After I'd put the cheque into my bank, Henri persuaded me to return to France. They were holding a reunion for our old resistance group. I never considered myself as working to save France and all that heroic patriotism that Paul had so passionately believed in. For me it was a case of hating the Nazis and helping to rescue and save people from their evil. Against my better judgement, I went along to the meeting. There were faces I recognised and a lot of old friends of Paul's greeted me with kisses and said what a wonderful, brave person he was. During the formal speeches, I was shocked when the mayor stood up and announced they had named a street after him, Rue Paul Larouchamps and presented me with a Croix de Guerre. I was almost too embarrassed to receive it. No one had said anything about it beforehand. I made a little speech about cherishing Paul's memory and how humble I felt but deep inside I felt like an imposter, knowing so many comrades had paid a much higher price for our freedom. Going back was something I knew I could only do once. I went down to the old port, to the quiet street and stood in front of Paul's enamel plaque de rue. I used to think that life owed me something, but in the end the best thing you can do is live your life every day in your own way. C'est la Vie. I looked around for a quaint little chocolate box cottage and have been here ever since, helping out in the community whenever I can."

Eve turned to us and smiled. "You know, you two bright young things look great together. Max and Byrney, it has a ring to it like Bonnie and Clyde. You have to take every opportunity that comes your way, don't let life dictate to you; don't be afraid to make your own mark; that's my advice. The war was so long ago, it doesn't even feel like it happened to me, my life became very ordinary. I know you're keen to join the RAF Byrney, but I wouldn't if I was you. We may live in peaceful times now, but there will always be wars. I've seen at first-hand what man is capable of doing to his fellow man, believe me; it's not worth making such sacrifices." I stood up and completely lost my balance, just managing to fall back in my chair. Max began laughing hysterically which set Eve off in giggles too. The booze had crept up on me.

"What did you put in those drinks Eve? My legs have gone weird." Eve looked a little bashful and then out of concern said,

"I think we'd better order you a Taxi." I'd also not realised how dark it had become outside. The room was a little hazy too and Eve's ashtray was overflowing with tab ends and white ash.

"Probably not a bad idea." I was half laughing myself, as I tried to get my legs to work. Max stayed behind to help put things away whilst I sat in the taxi, with Eve's story still spinning around my head. I was amazed, not just by how much a person can pack into their life but how looks can be very deceiving too. Eve wasn't some dizzy, eccentric old lady that she appeared to be at work. I felt quite close to her, especially now that I knew her courageous and sad story.

I saw my Mums head appear through the lounge curtains as they parted and closed, briefly illuminating the empty parking space where my Moped should be right now. I practised aloud a few words, as I walked along our short path, attempting to square up my mouth, so that I wouldn't sound as pissed as I felt. But Mums are rarely fooled and my lob-sided grin was a bit of an easy giveaway for someone of Mum's experience.

"Sowwy Mum! I got a bit cawwied away listening to stowies about the waw."

"Just like your father! Always an excuse, it's like history's repeating itself here too! I think you'd better get to bed and don't think you'll be sleeping it off all day tomorrow either!"

"I suwwender," I said, as I slid open my bedroom door. I lay on top of my bed for a few minutes but the bedroom ceiling kept spinning, even with my eyes closed. I felt like I was crossing the Bay of Biscay in a hospital ship. It's all in the mind I said to myself, trying desperately to keep the contents of my stomach in place.

Chapter 6

A Few Day's Off

It was two days before I walked back to Crowston, to collect my Moped. It was in exactly the same place as I'd left it, next to Edward's car; the only difference was a couple of fresh pigeon splats, one on my seat and one on the tank. I was feeling almost back to normal. Yesterday's hangover had been horrendous and Mum had decided my punishment as having to creosote the garden fence panels at the back of our mobile home. But I survived and after a steady walk into Crowston, my body was feeling less like a bowl of jelly. I popped into the Friary shop, bought a can of coke and checked the weekend rota. Good, the usual Saturday crew: Max, me, Vicky, Frances, Hazel, Rhonda and Kevin. Outside, I knocked my coke back and was going to retrieve my helmet from my top box and there in the corner of my eye I saw Fionn leaning out of the lounge window.

"Blimey, you're always eating, Fi" I joked.

" What have you been doing?" she replied. "Noticed your bike's been parked up a while."

"Had a bit too much to drink the other night and took a Taxi home."

"Are you and Max going out together now?"

"Erm.. Who told you that?"

"Max came in the shop yesterday, looking as bad as you."

I didn't think I looked that rough today. "Should have seen me yesterday." I said, pulling a face and pretending to stagger.

"Why don't you come in a minute, you can share my ice cream."

"Yer why not?" Madge and Edward's lounge was decorated with tired but comfortable old furniture that they'd probably inherited at the time of their wedding, working on the theory that it must have been around seven years ago, as their two young children, Janie and Joey, were six and four years old respectively. The sun was shining in through the long, Georgian sash windows and the remnants of Fionn's meal sat on the oak coffee table. We sat together in the shaded part of the room on the big, spongey sofa. I picked up a spare tea spoon from Fionn's tray and took a scoop of her strawberry ice cream sundae. I gave her a very brief account of my visit to Mrs Herbert's, but Fionn was more interested in my budding romance with Max. "There's nothing much to tell, honestly. We've only met a couple of times. I'm happy we just get along together. I keep thinking she's going to dump me because I'm younger than she is."

"Don't be silly." Fionn replied. "What difference does it make and besides she told me she thinks you're really good looking."

"Yer! What else did she say?" At last I was going to find out how Max felt about me.

"She says you make her feel good."

"And?" I was hoping for lusting after my body

"Well, that she fancies you a lot."

"You're making it up!"

"Well you know Max. Always plays her cards close to her chest. I can tell though, woman to woman, she thinks a lot about you." The door creaked open and Joanie stuck her head in and said,

"Madge is asking for you Fi, time to finish off and get back to café." "Hi Byrney, feeling better now?" she added, whilst shaking her head in amusement.

"Blimey does everyone know?" Joanie disappeared smiling. "I'd better be off myself anyway. You'd better not keep Madge waiting, otherwise she'll be blowing a gasket." Fionn took away her tray, laughing as she went.

"See you Byrney."

I didn't fancy going back home just yet, in case Mum had more hellish jobs waiting for me, so I decided to take a detour round to Marsh, to see if Lewis was in.

Lewis's parents had a nice, big detached farmhouse surrounded by fields and pasture. The sad looking fields with their withering crops of rapeseed, smelt of rotten cabbage, such a change from earlier in April, when they had gleaned bright yellow, like a Van Gough painting. I headed up the long driveway. I could see Lewis's blue Suzuki AP50 parked up outside his cabin. His cabin was actually very palatial. It must have been at least fifty foot long, larger too than our mobile home. Inside, he'd a full size snooker table and luxury of luxuries, a working jukebox. As I pulled opened the door. Lewis was playing snooker by himself and by the music I could hear, he was still going through his Status Quo phase.

"Fancy a game then?" I shouted, above the level of the record, making Lewis jump at my sudden appearance.

"Jesus Byrney! Didn't hear you come in." Lewis re-racked the snooker balls, while I made a couple of selections on his jukebox, 'Let's stick together by Bryan ferry and Peter Frampton's 'Show me the way'. Lewis flipped a coin as I chalked up a cue from the rack.

"Heads"

"Heads it is"

"I'll let you break." I said smiling. Lewis bent down, pulled back his cue and split the reds open, scattering them onto three cushions. Nothing down.

"Guess what?" he said

"Go on."

"Shagged Janet Johnson last night"

"No way, where?"

"Took her for a spin and we did it behind a wall in a field."

"Ha, you dirty bugger!" I was feeling quite envious as I'd not actually got that far with anyone yet, mostly my own fault. I always chickened out. I wanted to, but hadn't the nerve to ask. I think I was possibly the last virgin amongst my mates. "What did you say to her?" I cringed to myself, as this has to be the dumbest thing I've said so far this week.

"Nothing, we just got frisky as fuck and one thing lead to another and she just let me. Got through a pack of three."

"Bollocks!"

"Straight up! I'm going round to hers again tonight," he said grinning and waving a another pack of Durex, from out of his shirt pocket. Lewis beat me hands down at snooker, for some reason I was having difficulty concentrating.

When I rolled home again, Mum was in the kitchen, rushing round and setting the table for four. That's very optimistic I thought.

"Hi Mum, what's for tea?"

"I'm doing a Vesta curry, getting a bit fed up with salad all the time. There's a melon in the fridge if you want to help me? You can slice it up for starters."

"Will father be joining us?" I said sarcastically

"Your guess is as good as mine, but I've set him a place in case he turns up." I admired her loyalty. She could have done a lot better for herself than my Dad. Mum always said what a catch he was when he was young, good looking, steady job, his own car! That was before he got a taste for boozing at lunchtime. "It says on the BBC weather forecast that it's going to be the hottest day on record tomorrow, 97 degrees Fahrenheit" Anthony came in through the main door with a bright red face, having just finished his evening paper round.

"Get yourself a glass of water Anthony," said Mum, looking all concerned. "You look like a beetroot."

"Hi Ant!" I said. Our Anthony was a lad of very few words. He'd traces of melted chocolate around his lips. He could never resist buying sweets. He went through phases of eating the same chocolate bar for about three weeks, then he'd changed to a different one. Judging from the number of wrappers scattered about his bedroom, his current bar of choice was an Aztec. By the end of his weekly chocolate intake he probably owed the Newsagent more than he received in wages. I nipped his arm as he went past and he squealed "Lay off!"

"Don't start you two, and go and wash your hands Anthony," said Mum in a flap. We sat down to a runny curry and runny rice and a glass of warm Vimto. "What have you been doing all afternoon? I notice your bike's returned at last."

"Just been round at Lewis's, playing snooker. Anyone rung for me today?" Wondering if Max had called.

"Not while I've been in there hasn't. Why? Are you expecting a call, from a little bird perhaps?"

"No, just thought work might have rung that's all," I said, hiding my disappointment. Mum went over to the kitchen sink and started filling the washing up bowl. Then, looking out of the kitchen window, she said,

"Look at the state of our lawn. Brown and crisp and no one's allowed to use a hose pipe either. I don't know why we bother." It was a shame. Mum loved her little garden. Always growing flowers from seed and placing them in trays at the bottom of the airing cupboard, every spring time with such high hopes.

By 7.30pm Dad had still not appeared, so we sat in the lounge in front of the T.V watching Top Of The Pops. This was something the three of us had done ever since Mum had pinned up a picture of Dusty Springfield on my bedroom wall, when I was a young kid of seven or eight. Looking back, I was luckier than our Anthony, who was left with Cilla Black every night, no wonder he had nightmares. Most of my current favourite songs were slipping down the charts, so no chance of hearing them this evening and there was never any mention of punk on the BBC. The nearest thing we had was Thin Lizzy's 'Boys Are Back In

Town', but I found the lyrics to be too corny for my taste. This week's new entry to be featured was Paul McCartney's band, Wings and a song called 'Let 'Em In'. When the film started up to accompany the song, showing Paul and Linda and their kids getting out of planes and driving in big American cars, Mum - who always had a soft spot for The Beatles - said, "Arghh doesn't it make a refreshing change to see a pop star who's not wearing black eye liner and looking off his head on drugs." I guess they did look kinda ordinary for Millionaires, but I did enjoy listening to their catchy song, with lyrics referencing famous people. The weirdest thing ever was the new number one. Some fat Greek guy, in a white dress, called Dennis, didn't sound very Greek to me and his voice sounded like he was sat on a cactus.

"I'm off out for a bit Mum," I said, before the song ended.

"Where are you going?"

"Just round about."

"Well don't be late."

I found myself riding down Gunford Lane on the way to Crowston. I'd not arranged to meet up with Max, but just thought I'd have a ride over on the off chance she was in. As I rode past the rec, the swings were empty, so I carried on down Hook Lane, passing her house, which was in gloomy darkness - no one home. Okay, I thought, I'll keep going and maybe stop off at The Star. I pulled into the entrance and there were the usual gathering of shiny Rovers and Triumphs parked up beside the pub. I stopped the engine and just sat there on my bike, looking to see if I recognised anyone drinking at the outdoor tables. The ever present sun was still up in the sky, but the lengthening shadow from the pub was beginning to creep across the beer garden. Half a dozen crows caught my attention, pruning their feathers as they perched on the telephone lines that ran parallel to the road. In the field at the back of the pub a farmer had a motley crew, stacking bales of hay onto a flat wooden trailer. Watching them was giving me a thirst. I checked my pockets for loose change; there was plenty for a coke. I put my right arm through my helmet and carried it inside. I was waiting for my drink to be poured when I felt a tap on my shoulder. I looked around but it was the wrong shoulder; at the other side stood, oh no! Julie Nugent.

"Hello rude boy, I'll have a Slimline Tonic." She'd more money than I'd had hot dinners and she wanted me to buy *her* a drink.

"And a Slimline Tonic, please," I said to the barman, panicking I'd not enough money on me.

"One pound thirty," I had one pound fifty; that was lucky.

"How's your Dad?" I asked, as we remained standing at the bar. She frowned dumbly. "The Punk Party the other week?"

"Oh my God yes, sorry. He had to have his stomach pumped out. It was so embarrassing. Next Birthday I'm going away for the week." She looked around and reached into her handbag for a long brown cigarette that looked like a twiglet. "I suppose you're looking for Max," she said and lit up her twig cigarette with a silver lighter.

"No, not really, just happened to be passing."

"I think she's been having trouble with her Mum." That wasn't news to me, but I didn't let on to Julie that I knew, so I thought I'd do a little digging around.

"Where's Max's Dad when all this is happening?"

"Don't suppose she's told you, so you didn't hear this from me. Come on, let's sit down." We walked across to a quiet corner and sat opposite one another. Blowing her cigarette smoke through thick pouted red lips, Julie continued,

"Her father was a proper bastard to her as a child. He was always lashing out at her. Her Mum denied it was happening of course, until he started knocking her about as well. In the end, they walked out, well, ran away. They had an acrimonious divorce and afterwards she had to get a restraining order against him. Max and I used to talk about it at school. I got the impression it was just his fists he was using on Max. I don't think she ever forgave her Mum for the way he treated her. Please don't go repeating any of this to Max, will you? She's such a love; we've been best friends a long time.

"No I won't say anything." Does explain a lot I thought. "She never speaks to me about her family."

"That's Max for you. Keeps it all locked up inside. Would you like another drink?" Julie bent down and rummaged through her handbag making it obvious she lingering too long and allowing me to have a good eyeful down her cleavage. Bloody hell; she's a bit full on, I thought.

"No thanks, Julie. I've got to be off, early start tomorrow." I grabbed my helmet and stood up.

"If you see Max tell her I've been asking after her. Actually don't, I'll probably get in touch with her over the weekend." It was dark again outside, when I left the pub, but the car park was well illuminated, keeping the posh cars in good care. There were still a couple of hardy drinkers sat at one of the wooden bench/tables but, it was all quiet in the field behind, even the fussy crows had found a tree to roost in for the night.

Chapter 7

Max's Proposition

Hanging inside my wardrobe, was my favourite, leather bomber jacket. I'd bought it in Blackpool from one of the many well stocked, back street, leather shops. The shop was very basically set out inside, just a few rails packed with new jackets, all marked up at the same price, twenty pounds. If the shop hadn't had a glass front door you could easily be fooled into thinking you were stood inside the back of a lorry. I chose a loose fitting one, with a brass zip front, collarless and elastic waist band and in black of course. This was the ultimate fashion statement in Americana, just like Steve McQueen or David Starsky.

'Our gang of four had ridden over to Blackpool one evening after school about six months ago. It was just a spur of the moment thing: John, Andy, Lewis and me, all on our Mopeds. We made the obligatory stop off at the Kawasaki Showroom at Poulton traffic lights, drooling and dreaming over which machine we were going to move up to when we were seventeen. The KH250 triple, the 'Green Meanie' was a clear winner. After catching a couple of high street shops before they closed, we had a fish and chip supper at the Bus Station café. It had been almost dusk when we'd arrived, so by the time we left, it was pitch black and starting to rain. The journey back to Lewis's cabin was made through gritted teeth and a misty visor. We hung up our wet coats and began playing snooker. Lewis had some homebrew on the go, which went down very well. Lewis's parents were obviously a lot more liberal minded than mine. John had found a taste for the soapy looking beer, so much so that I had to deliver him home on the back of my bike as he was too drunk to ride his own'.

The leather jacket is now part of my uniform. I take it off the hanger and pull down the zip. They're a few scuffs on the elbows, but it looks better every time I wear it. I'd fallen out with my Brutus flared jeans ever since I'd slash the knees in my black drainpipes. I pick up a clean tea-shirt, put on my shark tooth neckless and lace up my blue, Adidas trainers. It was like putting on a suit a armour ready for battle. I lie on my bed, fully geared up and set my alarm clock for the following morning. It's difficult to describe a Friday night feeling, the tingling expectation, the pre-conceived preparation, thinking about who you might meet up with, playing your favourite records before you leave, no other night of the week feels the same. I take a Five Pound note from my jar in the bottom of my wardrobe and grab a handful of change. I check my visor, give it a quick clean with a handkerchief, final check in the mirror in the hall, head down and run my fingers through my hair. I hear a horn pip outside and my Mum shouting to me from the lounge that one of my mates is here. I check the window, to see the silvery blue fuel tank of an AP50, Lewis.

"See yer Mum"

"Just be careful on your bike!"

Lewis is sat astride his Moped resting his helmet on his fuel tank.

Lewis "Green Man?"

"Okay I'll follow you." And off he goes.

It's dead inside the Green Man at Brock. Andy and John were already sat in the corner next to the silent jukebox, so there was just the four of us, not surprising really as the pub has only been open ten minutes. We were about to raise our full pint glasses for the first taste when the door rattled open and in walked a Police

Motorcyclist. He looked about seven foot tall and completely humourless, in his shiny leathers, belted boots and check trim around his white helmet. He strode over to the bar and struck up a conversation with the landlady. It looked like he'd ordered a drink but it was hidden from our view.

"What do we do?" said John, his face whiter than the policeman's helmet. Our four full pints of bitter were sat on our table like hilltop beacons. "I'm not touching my pint, he's obviously clocked our Mopeds out the front, so he knows we're only sixteen."

"Well he hasn't turned round so I don't think he's seen us," murmured Lewis. We sat there for a long five minutes, staring at the copper who was still stood with his back to us.

"Bollocks to this!" said Andy, "I'm supping mine. If he wants to book us, let him." I looked at John who was still in a state of fear, then Lewis followed Andy's lead.

"If you can't beat 'em, join 'em" and smiling as he grabbed his pint and took a massive swig. The Policeman turned round and left, not paying us any attention whatever.

"He's probably waiting for us outside." said John still panicking.

"Nah!" disagreed Lewis.

"Game of pool anyone?" I picked up my pint at last.

The Moorcock at Bleasdale had the most lenient attitude to underage drinking to any other pub we knew. Most of the locals drank there with their children and as it was so remote it was very rarely visited by the local Constabulary, the nearest Police Station being about five miles away. It was not only lenient, but had regular 'Lock-In's'. I think there must have been some arrangement with the local 'Bobby', who never paid for a pint when he was off duty. Friday nights were more like a youth club than a pub. Sometimes there was a DJ, with coloured flashing lights, but most of the time the music came from the jukebox, volume set at ten and the lads and lasses tended to congregate at opposite tables. I knew a couple of girls from The Friary that were standing at the bar. I grabbed Lewis's collar and we walked over. Sue (the quiet tall one) and Julia (the noisy little one) were drinking pints of cider. I'd only worked with them on a couple of shifts, so conversation was limited to work. I could hear Andy's snarl at the other end of the pub - as some suicidal fool was making eyes with Tracey. Andy was having none of it.

"Outside now, yer Bastard." He was pushing this poor innocent farmer in the chest. "Yer were fuckin staring at her!" The lad backed away quickly and departed. "And that goes for the fuckin lot of yer an all!" I wasn't going to be the one to calm Andy down when his gander was up. Luckily, Tracey put an arm around his waist and they sat down, Andy's legs wide apart, his fists still clenched tight like mallets. I turned to Lewis,

"He gets worse."

"Nah, he's all talk, sweet as a daisy really," chuckled Lewis

"I'll let you tell him that."

"There you go, look, they're holding hands now."

"Well don't stare at them. Your round!" I said, wagging my empty glass. It was still quite early and the pub was filling up nicely I thought I'd risk another pint, that'd be my third.

The alarm sounds, decibels louder than usual. I roll over and thump the plunger. My head was thumping too. I look at my clothes in a pile in front of my wardrobe and thought about something Andy had once told us, about the after effects of drinking too much. You wake up to find a bear has visited you in the night. 'He throws yer clothes on the floor, kicks yer in the head then shits in yer gob'. I need an Alka Seltzer, fast. Dad normally has a tube in the kitchen, clink, clink, fizz, fizz. Just for a change the sun is streaming in though the lounge window.

I was making a very bad job of sweeping the carpet at work. I sit down on one of the café chairs and Vicky began tut-tutting at me and gave me an unsympathetic look. Max is brushing away. "Did you see the news last night? All those ladybirds swarming on the parked cars down Bournemouth or somewhere, billions of them?"

"Yes I saw that and if you don't get up quick Madge will be swarming all over you." replied Vicky, pausing for a moment.

I decided to skip the windows and go out into the backyard to do a couple of buckets of chips, grabbing a can of coke of the shelf as I passed through the passageway behind the kitchen. I was sat having a crafty break, whilst the potato peeler is drumming around, scraping away at their jackets. Just then the back door opens, I jumped up in case it's Edward, but it was just Kevin. Kevin lit up a fag, offers me one, then remembered I don't smoke. I took a swig from my can then placed it back behind the drum, out of view. Kevin began flattening a few boxes. He turned around and said, "Do you know if Vicky is going out with anyone?"

"Why do yer fancy her?"

"Yes, don't you, she's well tidy." I'd got to know Vicky a little over the years. Kevin was right she was tidy and good-looking too. I knew Vicky wanted someone more mature than me, but also I think I was a bit beneath her in her eyes. The only class we had in common was at school.

"No, I don't think she's seeing anyone at the moment, go for it, only don't mention you support Blackpool."

"Cheers Byrney," said Kevin, his head down and taking me literally. I thought Kevin would actually be a good match for Vicky. He was a couple of years older than me, more mature and he had one big advantage, he had his own car! Madge was waiting for me in her apron and black rubber gloves, hopping impatiently, next to the fryers. She had an order in her hand.

"Have you done the windows yet?" I was about to lie to her then thought better of it. "Leave them this week. Do you know how to fry eggs?" I'd seen Madge drown eggs in the frying pan.

"Yes?"

"Well here's an order for egg and chips twice, you can have a go at cooking it." Then she walked up the steps into the shop and left me to it. Vicky, who'd been listening in, looked up at me from 'marjing up' her loaves of bread. I shrugged my shoulders at her.

"You're Madge's blue-eyed boy," she said.

"Oh god, don't say that," and we both laughed. I pushed the eggs around the frying pan to make sure they were well submerged in cooking oil and didn't stick to the bottom. A batch of chips were already steaming away in the fryer behind me.

"Is this one of your orders Hazel?" I shouted as she entered the kitchen, "Egg and chips, twice?" She looked at me gone out.

"Does Madge know you're messing about with her orders?" Madge appeared at the top step between the kitchen and the shop with her gloved hands on her hips.

"Yes she does Hazel. Now, let's have a look at those eggs. Nice and evenly cooked, well done Byrney, we'll make a chef out of you yet. Right, have you all decided what you're having for you lunches?"

We took up our usual position at the long table above the gift shop. Max was sat in her usual position too, at the head of the table, eating a salad sandwich that had been cut diagonally into quarters. Kevin had parked himself next to Vicky and was telling us all how he'd fitted a black, eight ball for a knob on his gear stick (good job Miss Nugent wasn't here I thought, she would have had a field day with that). I looked across at Max, smiling to herself. I could tell she was thinking the same too.

" You drill down into the pool ball and the tricky bit is cutting the thread," Kevin explained. Vicky looked impressed. Max was pulling faces at me and as we all got up to go back to the kitchen,

Max grabbed my arm and when everyone else was out of earshot, said she had a proposition for me.

"Blimey I know it's a leap year Max but it's a little sudden," I said joking. She purposefully ignored my remark and continued,

"I can't talk about it here. Can you come back to my house this evening after work?" I wasn't sure what to make of it, but what else could I say? I saw in her eyes she was deadly serious.

"Got something up your sleeve?" I said

"You'll have to wait and see." Sounding more like her usual self.

Back in the kitchen Madge was in full flow. She had a polythene bag of pork chops that she was slamming down on the floor. Here we go again I thought. Everybody's eyes were dancing up and down.

"Remind me never to eat here again," I said to Max.

"That's nothing! I've seen Madge jump up and down on them before now." Beats having to tenderise them I thought. The kitchen radio was tuned into radio one, as usual for a Saturday. At 3.00pm it was the American Billboard Top One Hundred, presented by Paul Gambaccini. This was where I'd first heard Steve Millers fantastic album. The songs on the American charts were much the same as the English charts, but Gambo always made a point of saying how difficult it was for English bands to be successful across the pond.

When I next came into the kitchen Madge was singing along to the Dr Hook love song, 'A Little Bit More' I was making up a tray, trying not to look back at her but when she sang the chorus '...when your bodies had enough of me and I'm laying flat out on the floor, when you think I've loved you all I can I'm going to love you a little bit more...', I couldn't get the picture of her and Edward canoodling on their sofa together out of my mind. It was worse than imagining your own Mum and Dad at it. I must have been stuck in a daydream, or was it a nightmare? when Madge suddenly broke off from her singing to bark out loud,

"If you don't get that tray into the café in the next ten seconds I'll squeeze your bum." I was out of the kitchen in a flash. Madge was still laughing when I came back in. "Don't look so hurt Byrney, I was only joking." Joanie was filling up a pot of tea and trying not to laugh. Luckily, this amorous scene was interrupted by one of Edward's timely visits to the kitchen.

Edward was studying Madge, "Everything alright my Sweet?"

"I was just threatening to squeeze Byrney's bum if he didn't get a move on," she replied.

" I should do as she says," agreed Edward, disappearing back to the gift shop with his mug of tea; he whispered to me "Fate worse than death."

It was funny moments like these that made working at The Friary so enjoyable. It's true the atmosphere could be very fraught at times, even when things were at their busiest and we were having to rob dirty trays for bowls of sugar and condiments; everyone just adapted and got on with it, seeing the job through to the end. It was a real mental marathon just keeping track of all the orders, making sure they added up and no one got the better of you.

At the end of the shift Max had seven neat piles of coins from the tips jar waiting for us.

"I'll wait outside for you," I said, as I put my pile of coins inside my jacket. Ten minutes later I was pushing my Moped along next to her. And once we were out of sight of the shop, I said, "Jump on, I'll give a ride down to your place. Don't worry I won't go fast." Max stretched over the seat behind me, no helmet of course and she put an arm around my waist. We pulled into her drive, came to halt and as Max hopped off, her Mum came out of her front door and walked up to her car.

"I'll pretend I didn't see that." she said with daggers for eyes, aimed in my direction.

"Oh, hi Mum" said Max.

"I'm going to Gerald's for the evening, he's having a little soiree"

"That'll be nice" I heard Max say sarcastically, as I stored my helmet inside the top box. The MG car door slammed shut and roared out of the drive.

"Come on Byrney, let's go inside" as soon as the front door closed, Max kicked off her shoes. "Can I get you anything? A drink, or a beer?"

"Yer please, I could murder one!"

"Go on up to my room, put some music on, I'll be up in a minute."

Max's room was organised chaos. The drawers of her dressing table were all half open and various items of underwear were strewn across the floor. I thought about picking them up, but bent down to flick through her LP's instead. There was a lot of female singer songwriters like Joni Mitchell, Carole King and Carly Simon. I noticed 'Fly Like An Eagle' was still sat on her record player, so I flipped it over onto side two and switched it on: 'This is the story 'bout Billy-Joe and Bobbie-Sue...' Max was stood in the doorway, holding two cans of Colt 45.

"I noticed you like this, so I bought some in for you," and there she goes again with that fantastic smile of hers. "Don't worry about all the mess. I'm normally neat and tidy, but leave it all lying about to annoy Mum."

"She didn't look that impressed with me just now either," I said and sounding eager, "So come on then what's this proposition?" I pulled off my ring pull and knocked back some cold beer.

"Funny you putting this track on, it's a little ironic," she said, listening to the lyrics '...two young lovers with nothing better to do...' "What would you do with ten thousand pounds?" she announced rather abruptly. My heart skipped a beat,

" Ten thousand pounds! You've got me there Max, what are you talking about?"

I listened to Max's proposition, not sure if I'd 'entered the realms of fantasy' or not. At first I thought it was a joke, robbing the Post Office, here in Crowston. She had the whole plan figured out. When we were round at Eve's last week, after I'd gone, Max had stayed behind a while longer and Eve let it slip that she was minding the Post Office, while Brian and Rita were away on holiday for the week. It also coincided with it being the Monday before late Summer Bank Holiday and there would be at least twenty thousand pounds in the safe, as that day would be a double issue of child allowance and pensions.

"So what, we just go in there and hit Eve over the head and steal the money? You must be crazy!"

"No, it would be a cinch. We wouldn't have hurt Eve, just tie her up before she opened the Post Office." Max spread out her arms and looked down at me. "Do you want to work all your life, in all that drudgery, all that nine to five stuff? Well not me!"

"And what happens when we get caught?"

"Look Byrney, I've had a real scary, shitty childhood. My father was a violent monster and my Mum has never loved me or stuck up for me. There were times when I would rather have been dead." Max was beginning to tremble with emotion. I'd never seen her like this. She took a big swig of her beer and regained her composure. "Things happened to me as a child, horrible things." I was beginning to feel quite bad and wanted to let Max know I was on her side, but she put her hand up to silence me. " Some things I just can't talk about. You trust me don't you Byrney?" I put my arms over her shoulders and looked into her eyes to find the Max I thought I knew.

"I love you." I wasn't sure if it was the right thing to say, but I meant every word. "But I'm not sure this is such a good idea.

What if it all goes wrong and something happens to Eve?" Max pulled away from me slowly and switched off the music.

"You know I like you a lot and afterwards I'd like us to go away together, somewhere beautiful, just the two of us. Think about it Byrney, please!" That was some bombshell. I was trying to take it all in. I made up an obvious excuse to leave and Max followed me downstairs and then we kissed. I could tell Max was regretting opening up to me.

"I'll give you a ring in a couple of days." I was trying not to sound hollow and disappointing. As I rode home, I couldn't think of a way that Max's plan would work. It seemed such a hare-brained scheme. Max was far more intelligent than I was, but the more I thought about it, the more I dismissed it. What I couldn't get out of my mind was thinking about Max's desperate childhood, all alone with no one to protect her. I wanted to stand beside her; I'd fallen for her big time.

I decided to empty my brain at home, watching TV with Mum and Anthony. Dad was down the pub, as usual and he was missing out on some serious, Saturday night entertainment, 'Starsky and Hutch'. The program had just finished, when our phone began to ring.

"Ten o'clock at night, who's ringing up at this time?" said Mum as she picked up the phone. "It's your father, says he wants a word with you," and she handed me the phone. I listened to Dad's voice which sounded unusually sober,

"One of your mates has been badly injured outside the Chippy in town. There's a right commotion going on. Think you'd better get yersen down here." I put down the phone, flew into the kitchen and grabbed my helmet.

"Hey, hey calm down, what's going on?" said Mum looking all concerned.

"There's been a fight in town, one of my mates has been hurt, I'm going see if he needs my help."

"Well tell your father to get himself home then."

When I got to the chip shop the first thing I noticed was a huge crack in the big glass window. Two policemen had their hands full, wrestling with a man on the ground and I saw Lewis a few yards away, pacing about and swinging his helmet, shouting, "The fucking bastard!" I leapt off my bike and ran over to him.

"What's happened, mate!" I tried to grab hold of him to calm him down.

"It's Andy, he's fucking dead!"

"You're joking!" but clearly he wasn't. Lewis slammed his helmet against the wall.

"It was fucking awful Byrney"

"What's happed to Andy?" I grabbed hold of Lewis and sat him down on the kerb. An ambulance had just pulled up; I could hear a girl start to scream; it was Tracey, Andy's girlfriend. Another police car arrived, blue lights flashing, sirens wailing. A crowd of people stood opposite outside the Bulls Head, the drama unfolding in front of them as they stood staring, still holding their pints of beer. I could see my old man over there too.

Lewis, Andy and Tracey had been out drinking and afterwards Tracey wanted to take some fish and chips home for her Dad. Little did any of them know, Tracey's Dad was sat waiting in his car, opposite the chip shop. When they came out, he began threatening Andy. The night before, Andy and Tracey had had an accident on their way home from The Moorcock. Nothing serious, Andy had just over run a bend on his Moped and they'd gone straight through a hedge. When they arrived back at Tracey's, her Dad had gone ballistic, accused Andy of being reckless. To cut a long story short, he wanted Andy out of his daughter's life, permanently.

When they came out of the chip shop, Andy was up to his old tricks, goading Tracey's Dad as usual. He wasn't afraid of anyone, least of all him. They set to, but Andy hadn't seen the fucking huge kitchen knife, until Tracey's Dad plunged it into his chest, dragging it down and spilling Andy's guts over the pavement. Lewis made a lightning fast reaction, clobbering Tracey's Dad around the head with his crash helmet, almost knocking him out. Lewis sat on him until the police arrived. What a mess! I was shaking at the sight of all the blood on the pavement after the ambulance had gone, but God knows what Lewis was thinking. The police were taking names and addresses of witnesses. My Dad wondered over and said, "Come on lad, let's get home, there's nothing anyone can do now." I checked Lewis was okay. The police were going to take him home; they had taken his helmet away as evidence, so I said I'd see him some time tomorrow. In my young lifetime this had to go down as the worst thing to happen to a guy of my age, in our quiet, little West Lancashire market town.

The police van was just pulling out of Lewis's parent's driveway the following morning, as I turned to go up it on my Moped. I parked up outside Lewis's cabin and walked down the adjoining pathway to the side door of the house. Lewis's Mum saw me approach and let me in. "Hi Byrney come through to the lounge, Lew is sat inside." She lead me through the kitchen and into the hall way "That door there," she pointed.

"Thanks Mrs Coulter." Lewis was sitting on a brown leather Chesterfield sofa and staring at some Police victim support leaflets on the coffee table. I sat down in the armchair opposite, next to the green tiled fireplace and nodded at Lewis. "Mate."

"Bastards pleading self-defence, can you believe it? Bloody nutter!" he said bitterly.

"Is that what the Police said?"

"Yes, after I made my statement. I got a bit wound up. They said I shouldn't worry. He'll get what's coming to him. Said they had a witness who saw him sat in his car for a whole hour, outside the chippy. Bastard must have planned it from start to finish." Lewis was shaking his head slowly from side to side in disbelief.

"Can't get Andy's face out of my head. When he'd been stabbed, he never cried out, nor nothing. Just had this comical smile on his face then he just feel to his knees. That's when I walloped The Bastard with my helmet. It all seemed to happen out of nowhere. I could have jumped in and stopped it, but Andy thought he could take on the world. Now look at him! His life snuffed out, before he's even reached seventeen, he'd his whole life ahead of him."

I was thinking about all the people Andy had knocked over at school in the past, even kids who were in years above us. He was a bit of a thug really, who you didn't want to get on the wrong side of. There again, I didn't know him as well as Lewis. Either way, Lewis was right about one thing, he'd his whole life ahead of him; to think how suddenly it came to an end. For some reason I was thinking about Eve's husband Paul and how his life was taken away too and the mess that it left behind amongst the living. Some scars never heal, like guilt that goes unreconciled, because the dead can't speak. Most of all I was thinking about how one minute people were here and the next minute gone. It made me realise I had a big decision to make and that I needed to know how Max truly felt about me and that she wasn't just coaxing me along.

"Andy's funeral is probably going to be next week, are you going?" asked Lewis.

"Probably not, sorry mate, but I didn't really know him all that well. But if you want me to go with you?"

"Nah, leave it Byrney, can't say as I'm looking forward to going myself. I'll give you a call when it's over."

"Yer do that, we'll have a few pints, send him off in style eh?"

"See yer mate"

Chapter 8

A Day At The Seaside

Max was out when I knocked on her door. Her Mum couldn't close it fast enough. She'd no idea where she was. (Liar) So I rode down to the railway bridge, taking a chance that Max was out on her favourite walk. The afternoon sun was at its hottest. I couldn't remember the last time it had rained, not that I wanted it to, but the change would at least break up the monotony. Along the path, it felt like I was walking in a biblical plague. Next to me were dusty, dried stalks of corn creaking in the breeze and the grey soil beneath was set like badly mixed concrete. As I approached the river, the water level was a good twelve inches lower than it had been a week ago. Rocks were jutting above the surface like fossilised dinosaur teeth. What was happening to our planet; it looked like everything was dying of rainlessness. Up ahead I caught a glimpse of Max stepping over the stile. When I reached it, she leapt out from behind the wall.

"Boo!" she said, as I dropped my helmet. "Did I scare you?"

"Nah!"

"Thought I might see you today. Changed your mind?"

"About the robbery?" Max was shielding her eyes from the sun as I climbed over the stile to join her. "Before I say yes, I need to know what the plan is for afterwards? That is if we don't get caught." Max leapt forward again, this time throwing her arms around my neck and sowing kisses across my face. "Wait a minute Max, let's just sit down and talk it through."

Max began discussing the preparations, things I'd not even thought about, like changing the number plate on my Moped, gloves, stockings, rope... She knew the lay out of the Post Office, even where the back door was and how to get to it, what time Eve would arrive etc. etc.

"And afterwards what?"

"Well we carry on as normal, to avoid suspicion," said Max coolly. "You take care of the money, put it somewhere safe, then we hand in our notices at work and disappear into the sunset." I thought about what Max had just said for a while, as we sat on the riverbank, occasionally throwing pebbles into the green algae that lay on top of the motionless water. Max made it sound so simple.

"Promise me Eve won't get hurt."

"Eve's a lot tougher than she looks."

"Everyone keeps saying that but she's probably at home right now, coughing into her oxygen mask."

"No, I saw her in the village yesterday. She even waved at me."

"Okay, so I'll buy a fake number plate for my Moped?"

"Don't be silly. Let's steal one; it'll be more fun. Besides, shops keep records of number plates."

"You're mad," I said, laughing.

"Come on!" she said, "Race you to the swings." and she was off, before I'd even stood up.

"Cheat!"

We both sat side by side on the pair of swings, our toes touching the ground and we were gently rocking ourselves from side to side.

Max "What made you change your mind?"

"Last night, a guy I knew in town was murdered - knifed outside the Chippy.

Max put her hand on mind, " Gosh, how awful."

"You just never know what life has in store, one minute your buying supper.."

"...the next, you've had your chips," Max interjected, "sorry, that sounded crass."

"Exactly! It made me feel helpless and insecure. I want to live as far away from that as possible. Do you think ten thousand pounds would be enough to buy my own island?"

"No, but twenty thousand could be," said Max. It was as simple as that. We were a pair of dreamers with the same will to live our lives by our own rules - to hell with everyone else. We left the swings wrapped together and began walking through the village and down Hook Lane. The small electric street lamps had just begun to flicker, we could hear distant voices and the garbled sounds of TV's, homes with all their windows opened fully; some even had their front doors wedged open too. The evening still clung to a barmy temperature. Max put my hand in hers and squeezed them both into her pocket, smiling brighter than I seen her do in a while - don't ever change, Max. It was a perfect evening.

The following week, I was making a few plans of my own for the 'Post Office job', but at the same time still having doubts. One day I was all for it, the next I was convinced we were about to make a huge mistake. It seemed too simple, too good to be true. Half way through the week, my parents announced they were taking a week's holiday in Scotland, leaving a week on Friday. Anthony was going with them and they would like me to come along too. I made my excuse that I was needed for work as a lot of staff were also on holiday. To tell the truth, I really would have preferred to go with them. We'd had a couple of family holidays on the west coast of Scotland and on the Isle of Bute, twice before in the last five years and I really loved the peacefulness of the rugged Scottish coast line. I clearly remember Dad's words the first time when we'd arrived at the little hotel where we staying in Kilchattan Bay. He stopped the car, got out and said "Listen! You could hear a pin drop, it's so quiet". I suggested perhaps I could come up by myself, later in the week on my Moped. "Don't be stupid" was my Mum's only response. The thought of me riding the hundred and fifty miles to Scotland was more scary for her than me being alone here all week. I took it to be a good omen that everyone would be out of the way, now that Max had more pressing plans for me. 'Well there's still time for you to change your mind' is how my parents left it for the time being. Too true I thought, though it would be the end of Max and me if I pulled out now.

At the end of our garden stood our small wooden tool shed. It was a new addition when we arrived here two years ago. Dad had prepared the ground by laying a dozen concrete slabs in a six by two pattern. When the shed had been erected, it took up less room than he'd anticipated. I noticed, at the back of the shed, two slabs lying fallow, which were currently being used as a dumping ground; for bags of sand and some old fence posts. The two slabs looked about the same size as my old metal ammo box that was stored under my bed. The ground beneath the slabs would make an ideal place to hide the money, not that I'd any idea how big a space twenty thousand pounds would require. But if we're only taking two rucksacks with us, they would easily fit inside my ammo box. Sorted! I can start digging as soon as Mum and Dad have gone away.

The following Wednesday, I was stood next to my Moped, in the old truck stop car park, on the opposite side of the Main Road from the entrance to our mobile home park. It was a big, uneven stretch of ground, that had been ploughed over by many an articulated lorry in those days before the arrival of the new motorway, during the mid-sixties. This I had learnt recently from our elderly neighbours 'The Taylors' who'd told me back then our road had been the only route to link together Glasgow and the Midlands. The old Truck stop café building was still more or less intact, although empty and unloved. The windows were either broken, or boarded up. I was focussing on the bus stop and checking my watch, waiting for Max to arrive. We'd decided it would be a good idea to keep my visits to Crowston on my Moped, down to a minimum. When the bus from Lancaster eventually arrived, ten minutes late, Max stepped off and gave me a wave. Better late than never although under the circumstances, never might have been more preferable, given what Max had planned for today. I thought to myself, if I can't steal a number plate in broad daylight then it's hardly likely I could go through with robbing a post office, which is precisely what Max was probably thinking. Max walked towards me, like a catwalk queen, she didn't know it, but she looked amazing.

" Hi got everything we need?" she asked.

"Hi yes, two types of screwdrivers, spare helmet for you - bag of nerves for me."

"Good, where are we off to then?"

"Thought we should try Glasson Dock; there's bound to be loads of motorbikes there during the holidays."

"Great, how far is it?"

"Not far, about ten miles, jump on!" I looked again at what Max was wearing. "Haven't you brought a coat?"

Max looked at me, puzzled, "Why should I have? It's lovely and warm." That t-shirt she's wearing is hardly the most appropriate thing for a motorcycle journey.

"If you get too cold you'll have to hug up close" I said, noting she plainly wasn't wearing anything under her t-shirt either. It was quite a bendy old road, most of the way and with Max sat behind me, it took a while for me to get used to the changing weight distribution rounding the corners. We eventually arrived safely at 'The Dock' thirty minutes later.

I could see the car park at The Stork Inn was completely rammed with Motorbikes and Mopeds and also chocker-block along the road down to the Estuary. The ice cream van by the Estuary path was doing a roaring trade too. The queue was at least ten deep, when we joined the back of it. Directly in front of us in the queue, a middle-aged man, wearing a shirt and tie, was looking decidedly hot under the collar. He was holding hands with a pretty young girl, about six years old, in a spotted red dress. They were discussing what size ice cream to buy, The man, presumably her father, was trying to talk the little girl into settling for a single cone, rather than the double one that she had her heart set on. I looked at Max, who had also been listening to them and we both smiled knowingly at one another. The excitable little girl was clapping her hands at her own success, as the ice cream lady handed her a strawberry and chocolate cone. As they turned away, her father grabbed her hand, to guide her away and as she spun round her two blobs of ice cream fell on the floor and she immediately started to cry. Her father shouted, angrily,

"You stupid, little cow, what did I tell you!" and he made no attempt to console his daughter. Max jumped in, with both feet.

"How dare you shout at her like that; you ought to be ashamed of yourself." The man squared up to her, clenching his teeth. I was getting ready to jump in.

"Why don't you mind your own business you stuck up bitch," he replied. He bent down picked up the little girl and offered her his own ice cream and walked away with the girl still bubbling away in tears. Max called after him saying you shouldn't be anywhere near kids and that men like him ought to have a ring through their nose, which caused some laughter amongst the other people queuing. The man shouted back, with a single finger raised, "Piss off Bitch!" I could sense Max shaking with anger, or was it fear? I couldn't tell. We moved off in the opposite direction. Our appetite for buying an ice cream had disappeared.

"That's how it starts, shouting and bullying, next he'll be raising his fists to her, or worse." I could tell Max was speaking from experience; her expression was deadly serious.

I didn't know what else to say other than "Come on, let's go somewhere else."

There were too many people: hanging around in cars, on boats, fishing off the quayside. Max was still scanning the horizon for a sight of the bully. I made a point of checking the chin strap of her helmet to distract her. It also gave me the opportunity to look into Max's eyes. Her anger was easing and I kissed on the end of her pink nose.

"Let's try Cockerham Sands. Or we could always call it off for the day?" Max gave me a scowl. "Cockerham Sands it is then." Twenty minutes later, we were walking along, next to the beach, licking our ninety nine ice cream cones. Max had 'Monkey Blood' on hers too. We strode along the sea front, surveying the area for a potential donor number plate. At the end of the shoreline, we sat on the last wooden bench. It wasn't going to be as easy as I thought. Thanks to the static caravan site in the next field, there were hundreds of people all around. It was like a Bank Holiday Monday in Blackpool. We both heard a lone motorbike drive past and pull up fifty yards further up the path and watched, as a young couple took of their helmets and lock the steering. Looks promising, I thought, nudging Max with my elbow. The girl had a shoulder bag and the man retrieved a sports bag from his top box, then they walked over the nearest sand dune towards the sea. We nodded at each other and walked nonchalantly over, to see where they went. They were nowhere in sight. Then we heard some laughing, behind one of the dunes. We crouched down and moved closer. They were laying down, sunbathing on their towels and listening to a cassette player – 'Sheer Heart Attack', by Queen.

"Ok, you keep an eye on them and I'll go and get my tools."

Max rolled her eyes, "Where are they?"

"Still in my rucksack, inside my top box." I walked back and retrieved my rucksack and when the coast was clear, I dropped it behind the donor bike and pretended to tie my shoe laces, noting the size of the screws holding the number plate. I glanced round again. Max's silhouette towered above the grass tufted hump of a sand dune. She had one hand shielding her eyes and the other on her hip. She was stood, completely motionless, looking out towards the hazy, shimmering sea. What was she staring at?

I lowered my gaze to concentrate on the job in hand. Luckily there were no retaining nuts on the back of the screws and they loosened remarkably quickly, so quick that the number plate fell on the path. I nervously looked round and stuffed it straight into my rucksack. Max ran over and said excitedly, "Did you get it?" I just waggled my eyebrows, patted my rucksack and threw it over my shoulder. Immediately, a hand tapped me from behind. I froze with fear then came a familiar voice, "Aye up Byrney!" It was Lewis.

"What you doing here?" I said, forcing my words out.

"Just getting a bit of fresh. I needed to get out. Fancy a quick one?" Lewis pointing towards The Ship Inn.

"Max, this is Lewis, fellow Mopeder and drinking partner." Max stepped forward and shook Lewis's hand. Lewis gave me a look of approval.

"My round," he offered.

"Ok with you Max?" I said, as I locked my rucksack inside my top box. We went to find an empty table in the beer garden, whilst Lewis disappeared inside. On a sun soaked breezy day like this, the pub must have been doing a roaring trade, judging by all the empty crisp packets that were blowing under the tables and around the garden. Everyone seemed to be doubling up on their drinks for last orders. The caravan site next door looked to have double up on vans too; not a patch of green space remained.

"Just got these in time," explained Lewis, as he rested a tray down on our table with three pints of cider. "What you two doing all the way here then?"

"Fancied a ride out to Glasson dock, but it was heaving." I could see Lewis eyeing Max up and down, as he took a long slurp of his drink.

"Nice day for it," was all he could manage to say. I thought about asking how Andy's funeral had gone, but didn't want to spoil the day. It was Max who broke the silence.

"I take it you know one another from School? I'll bet your both glad to be free of all that?"

"I left at Easter, already working in the family building business so it was a no brainer for me," replied Lewis.

I was looking over towards the sand dunes in the distance and noticed the couple had returned to their motorbike. They were having an animated conversation and looking around for the culprit that had stolen their number plate. I instantly began to feel guilty - too late to turn back now Byrney. Max was looking at me, waiting for an answer to her question, "Hello," she said, trying to catch my attention, "You're thinking of joining the RAF aren't you?"

"Maybe."

The couple on the motorbike were leaving. I imagine they'll probably get stopped by the police on their way home, wherever that might be. Then I heard Lewis telling Max I'd still not lost my cherry!

"Bloody hell, cheers Lewis! Just ignore him Max," but she was already smiling away to herself.

"Just putting in a word for you Byrney"

Following my own advise I chose to ignore Lewis too and checked the time. "We'd better get going soon." I looked at Lewis again, who still had his gaze fixed on Max. "I'll give you a ring later in the week mate, see what you're plans are for the weekend."

"Yer, do that mate," and he raised his glass in salute. We walked by the side of the pub and down the path to where we'd parked up, earlier in the day.

"Your friend Lewis has a one track mind," said Max. "It felt like he was having a conversation with my chest the whole time."

"Yer, that's Lewis." Though I could see what the attraction had been for Lewis as I was doing my best not to stare at the two volume control buttons, pushing out Max's t-shirt.

Chapter 9

Countdown

When Friday morning came around early, Mum was going through her written notes with me: Here was the name and address of the hotel where they were staying in Scotland; it was a Mrs Gordon and there was her number, if I needed to call. Dad had left some instructions on how to change over the gas bottle. "And don't forget to switch everything off when you go out!"

He was beginning to get a sweat on, packing suitcases, golf clubs, picnic boxes, walking boots and raincoats into the boot of the car. It wasn't exactly fitting in well, so we all left him to it, to save having our heads bitten off. Anthony had a bag of sweets to last him the week, but he'd already started on them. Mum was threatening to take them away from him, as no doubt he would begin to feel car sick before they'd even reached the motorway. As I watched from the fringes of their departure, it appeared to me to be the usual organised calamity that accompanied us whenever we went away together. But this was my family and I knew I would miss them all and part of me wanted to be up in Scotland too. 'Don't forget to lock the door,' was their parting shot. I imagined Mum would be 'having pink kittens' all week, just worrying about me. Had I lost my key? Had I burnt our home down to the ground? etc. It's okay Mum, I'm only going to rob a Post Office.

I was sitting in the lounge with a cup of tea, listening to my Bowie Live double album on our old Garrard stereogram. I was thinking about Max, her outburst at Glasson Dock. I couldn't help thinking I should have backed her up, stepped forward to defend her. I hoped she wasn't thinking I'd let her down. I made a mental note to defend her honour in future. Outside, it was still very much shorts weather. Was there to be no end to the sunshine? Perhaps we heading towards oblivion after all. In the previous night's news on TV, it had showed clips of the Lake District. The water level at a reservoir there had dropped so low it had uncovered the muddy remains of a lost village. I was washing the dishes and looking at our neighbour's mobile home. The Taylors were gingerly walking down their steps, carrying some empty shopping bags, off for their weekly venture into town.

My thoughts were interrupted by a sound at the main door. It was only the local newspaper being delivered. I bent down to pick up The Courier. On the front page, was written the bold headline, 'Young Man Murdered On High Street'. Beneath it there was an old school photo of Andy, with his hard grin, top button undone on his white shirt and a loose tie, tied in a fat knot and with the tail of his tie, resting over his shoulder. The whole thing reminded me of a hangman's noose. I stared at the photo, picturing the last time I'd seen him, at The Moorcock, threatening to take on anyone who stared at his 'Bird'. The article made gloomy reading. Ron Birkhill, age forty-four, was in custody, until his hearing at Preston Crown Court next week. Witnesses had seen him sat in a parked car in the street, on several occasions earlier that evening. The article went on to say Andy had been a popular figure at school and there was even a quote from our headmaster, Old Beaver Face, saying Andrew Dunne had left school at Easter to start work at a Metal Recycling Plant. Further down, it mentioned Andy's girlfriend. Tracey Birkhill, age fifteen, who had been present when he'd died, was still in a state of shock and expecting a baby. So Andy had the last laugh after all. I wouldn't like to be in Ron Birkhill's shoes when he's eventually released from Prison to face Andy's twenty-five year old off-spring, stood waiting outside the gates for him. The article also mentioned Lewis's heroic actions in assisting the Police with the arrest of Birkhill. However, as there was an element of 'just cause' Birkhill's solicitor said his client would be entering a 'Not Guilty' plea. Reading the article made me all the more determined, rightly or wrongly, to take life by the scruff of the neck, but right now I'd a hole in the ground to dig.

Saturday morning I woke earlier than usual. I'd started a mental countdown, two days to go before we leapt blindly into the murky world of crime. There were still lots of things left to organise and the more I thought about it, the more nervous I became. The rucksack with the stolen number plate was still inside my top box. I needed to fix it to my Fizzie which meant having to drill new holes in my back plate. We'd decided it would be safer for me not to use my Fizzie for trips into Crowston during the week leading up to the robbery. So today, I was using my old faithful Sun racer bicycle, which I hadn't ridden for almost a year. When I took it out of the garden shed, both tyres were flat. I should have spotted this yesterday, when I was in here looking for a shovel. I borrowed Anthony's bike pump and luckily, the tyres inflated immediately. If I was quick, I'd still make it to work on time, especially if I took the short cut along Green Lane. I'd owned this bike all through senior school and it had never let me down. Dad had bought it second hand, over five years ago, from a pawn shop in Grimgate, for nine pounds. That was a memorable day - along with the time my bike had won me praise from the school deputy headmaster. Unknown to all the cyclists at school, on this particular day there had been a snap inspection by the Police Traffic Officer and my bike was singled out from the rest. When I came to retrieve it at lunchtime, it was leaning against the wall at the entrance to the bike shed and Mr Connolly was standing next to it, with a clipboard in his hand. As I approached, I spotted my bike had been moved. "Ah Byrne can you show me which is your bicycle?"

"Well it's this one you're stood next to," I said, looking mystified. Mr Connolly became instantly overjoyed with surprise and said,

"Well done Byrne. Yours is the only bicycle that doesn't have any faults at all." And off I pedalled proud as punch.

The Saturday morning routine at the café was becoming a chore I could do it with my eyes closed, on automatic pilot: carpets, windows, chips, boiled potatoes, Fatty and Thinny, then lunch. I'd not known it go this smooth before; there again I had been completely sober the night before, having stayed in alone watching TV and cutting out pieces of blue sticky back plastic. Fionn was in today, 'marjing up' the sliced bread and doing deserts for Vicky, who was away on two weeks holiday in Marrakesh, no idea where in the world that was; it just sounded like 'More Cash' which is what me and Max would have, this time next week.

It was a fairly ordinary afternoon. Gambo was on the radio doing the Billboard Top One Hundred. I always seemed to time being in the kitchen when 'Fly Like An Eagle' was playing. Madge was in a surprisingly good mood too. This was mainly because, she hadn't been interrupted all day by Edward - who was noticeably absent. I had a few awkward moments in the gift shop with Eve, who was doing her best to be friendly, but I found I couldn't look at her square in the face. She was very forgiving and even making fun about how good looking I was and that I should take Max away for a little holiday. If only she knew what we had in store for her. As it was fairly quiet, Madge suggested we take our afternoon tea in groups of three: Kevin and me to go first and whoever else would like to go at the same time? Fionn volunteered, which had Madge laughing hysterically. This woman is so strange I thought. As Madge handed us our tray she told Fionn to watch herself as Kevin and I would probably have her stripped naked in five minutes flat and said if she wasn't back in ten minutes, she'd send Joanie in to rescue her. It was all good natured banter, but I was still no wiser as to how Madge's mind worked. Upstairs, the usual cyclists were covering the tables with bread crumbs and tea stains. Max and I were able to see each other at our upstairs workstation. We agreed to meet up at twelve, midday the next day, outside the newsagent on opposite side of the village square, for a dry run and iron out anything we'd not thought of.

By 7.00pm, Edward still hadn't reappeared, so we all had to make our own way home. Kevin offered to take me up to The Star for a drink, but instead, I cycled back to Cayburn with Fionn.

"Have you had a letter from school Byrney? Our exam results are ready on Wednesday."

"No I bloody well haven't!" I was feeling taken aback as it was still really important to me. The last weeks at school had been really manic, doing extra lessons in the evenings and at lunchtime and for two or three nights before every exam, I'd confined myself to my bedroom and revised really hard. Being the eldest, Mum and Dad had given me a hard time to do well. Expectation was high.

" Maybe you'll get a letter on Tuesday. If you don't, just ring up the school and speak to the secretary."

"Good idea." I changed the subject, "Where the hell was Edward today? No one seemed to know."

"You'll never guess!" said Fionn "He was in bed all day! He had his wisdom teeth taken out yesterday. His mouth was really swollen and bloody when he came back from the Dentist. It was the first time I'd ever seen him speechless."

"Ha! Ha! Poor Edward," I laughed.

As we got to the bridge over the river, Fionn said,

"I'm going to have to get off and push my bike for a bit from here." I wasn't in any hurry, so I jumped off and walked beside her. We stared over the side of the bridge at what was left of the river, far below. It was a solid mass of green duckweed. There was a 'Private Fishing' sign by the stile - I wonder if the fish know they're trespassing too. Fionn said she was going to a dance at Barton Village Hall in an hour with her school friend, Jane Todd and would I like to go - her Mum was giving everyone a lift.

"I'd love to Fi but I'm meeting Max later," I lied.

"You've really got the hots for her. Be careful Byrney, she'll have a ring on your finger before you know it," she said, laughing at me. When we reached her house on Grant Road we went our separate ways, Fionn's was straight and true but where was mine heading?

Chapter 10

Stealer's Wheels

By the time I arrived at the newsagent the next day, I was uncomfortably hot and sweaty, having cycled over from Cayburn for the second day in a row. Max was waiting for me, wearing her customary short shorts, trainers and check shirt.

"Hi, I'd forgot you'd be on your bicycle." The newsagent was in the same row of terraced properties as the Post Office, which was at the opposite end and together they book-ended six, quaint, stone cottages. At the opposite end, I could see a familiar, round, red post box, with a black hat. Oddly there was a young girl sliding around on her belly on top of the post box, goodness knows what she was doing. I started to laugh.

"Right Byrney," said Max, "This is 'Operation Cool', take it seriously. First of all, we're not going to panic. Very little can go wrong."

"Oh you think? Eve is going to have a heart attack when she sees us rushing in with stockings over our heads."

"She'll have seen far worse than that in her time."

"Maybe, but not in Crowston!"

We walked past the Post Office which was closed and in locked darkness. The bottom half of the windows were frosted, so anyone stood outside had very little chance of seeing what was going on inside. Following the narrow footpath around the corner, Max pointed out the side gate that lead into the back garden. The tall, green, solid, wooden gate was set into a brick wall, about eleven feet tall and capped by overhanging stone slabs. I could see a brass Yale lock in the gate, which meant if you didn't have the key, it could only be opened from the inside.

"So how do we get in?" I enquired.

"Look at the end of the garden wall, the way that oak tree has grown over. It hasn't been cut back this year. Do you think you can climb over the wall by using the bottom branch?"

"That looks easy enough."

"Once you're over, you can open the gate and let me in. We can find somewhere in the garden to lie low until Eve arrives. Then we give her twenty minutes or so to put the kettle on and open the safe. That'll still give us half an hour before the shop opens at 9.00am."

"So what time do you think we should go over the wall?"

"Let's say 6.00am to be on the safe side; there won't be many people about then. You can park your Moped in the square, or the recreation ground by the swings."

"No," I said, " It's too open there. Let's walk further down here. We need to park my Moped out of sight. What about behind that hedge? Here, where this gate opening is leading into the field, perfect."

"Okay, I'll meet you here at 6.00am. Don't forget your rucksack and some gloves. I'll bring an old pair of nylon stockings. I think I'd much prefer to see Max wearing them on her legs, but didn't mention it to her, as it wasn't, 'Cool'.

"And some rope." I said. Max was looking around at the houses opposite. There was only a row of sleepy old folk's bungalows. "I can't see them giving us anything to worry about," I continued, as I followed Max's gaze. "There is one thing Max, say we get away with it and we go back to work and everything, then what?"

"Don't worry Byrney, we'll have plenty of time to make plans. Let's just concentrate on one thing at a time." And her smile beamed away at me.

"Tomorrow then!" I said.

"Don't be late!" Fat chance of that I thought, I'm going to be awake half the night just thinking about it.

Back home in the garden, I was transforming my Moped into Post Office getaway machine. On went the false number plate - I put my original one back in my top box - then the pieces of sticky back plastic (the kind you always see on Blue Peter, thanks Val), I'd cut them the night before. These were placed over the fuel tank and side panels covering up the bronze paintwork. There were a few spare pieces left over, so I did the same to both crash helmets for good measure. It wasn't a perfect job, but it would look fine from a distance. I made sure I'd enough fuel then threw over the rain sheet, to hide my Moped from nosey neighbours.

Sundays normally always dragged by, like an old lingering poem. If you wanted a drink, the shops were shut and the pubs shut at three in the afternoon until seven in the evening and not a drop to be had anywhere. For entertainment, there was only the one-day cricket match on the television so I decided to walk across to the estate and down Green Lane, to see if anyone was around. The walk took me past Fionn's house, but she was working at the Friary, Sunday being her normal day. No doubt all the cyclists would be giving her a load of cheek, as usual. The riverbank was quiet, not a soul around. It'd been weeks since the river was deep enough to swim in, putting a dam across it wouldn't help now either. The arid fields had been cut and the crops of hay gathered in, weeks ahead of schedule. I used to enjoy helping to gather up the hay bales in summer. Now, everywhere resembled a desolate dust bowl, begging for a few drops of rain. Even the Swallows looked cheesed off, as they sat scratching themselves on the high wire. Might as well head back myself, I thought. At the start of summer I'd plans to take myself on a road trip. Falling for Max had put an end to that innocent little adventure. Now that my dreams were bigger, how easy was it to turn fantasy into reality? I'd know the answer tomorrow. I was beginning to feel like we just might get away with it, if luck was on our side and if anyone deserved an ounce of luck, it was Max.

Eve was lying face down in a pool of her own blood. We were locked inside the Post Office, picking up five pound notes one at a time. Somehow, they had spread themselves all over the place, during the fight. Max was shouting at me to get a move on and waving a gun around. Where the hell had that come from? Then we heard knocking and angry voices at the front door. The large, electric wall clock, above the counter, was already showing more than ten minutes after opening time. We needed to find a way out and quick. We forced our way upstairs and smashed the bathroom window. I threw my rucksack to the ground, without aiming and noticed it had landed in the middle of a blackberry bush. I began to lower Max out of the window. Her hands were on the window ledge, next to tiny shards of broken glass. I could feel my grip on her sleeve slipping as the sound of the burglar alarm started up, louder and louder. I woke up sweating. It was my alarm clock. It was 5.30am.

I lay there a minute, still trapped within my nightmare. Thank god it was just a dream. I rinsed my face and took a long hard look in the mirror. No going back. I took a swig of orange juice, straight from the carton and put it back in the fridge. I had everything I needed laid out on the kitchen table. The spare crash helmet was in my rucksack, ready to hand to Max once we'd met up. A screwdriver and my original number plate were already inside my top box. I'd chosen to wear plain every day clothes: blue jeans, old jean jacket and my trainers. I thought it important not to look distinctive, in case we were witnessed at any stage. I closed our main caravan door behind me, turning the key - 'don't forget to lock up'. Outside in the garden, I pulled the rain sheet off my Fizzie and stuffed it behind the shed then, instead of starting up the engine, I pushed it the fifty yards or more out of the mobile home park. It was broad daylight, but eerily quiet. At a safe distance in the old car park, I started my Moped and headed up the Main Road, hoping not to meet any other vehicles. Instead of turning right down Gunford Lane, I carried on another three miles up the Main Road until I reached the other end of Hook Lane. Turning right, I headed down towards the river, that was partially erased by the cool, early morning mist that also clung to the outside of my visor, obscuring up my vision. Once I'd passed the railway bridge, I gave the throttle a quick blast of acceleration then I switched off the engine and coasted further down the lane. I saw Max waiting up ahead. I wheeled past and through the open gateway. I tucked my Moped close behind the hedge, facing back down the lane. Max was looking wide-eyed and whispered,

"All set?"

"Yes fine, so far, so good." We kissed each other and I handed her the spare helmet. She examined it quickly. I gave her my rucksack and my helmet too for her to carry.

"Right, you'd better get going. I'll be five minutes behind you." Max winked. I walked up the narrow path along the side of the lane, eventually focussing on the overhanging branches as they came into view at the end of the wall. The first one I grabbed snapped, making a sharp cracking sound. I jumped up to reach a higher branch that was strong enough to carry my weight. Using it as a lever, I walked up the wall horizontally until I could sit with my legs either side of the capping stones at the top. I crawled over the moss-covered stones for a few feet until I found a clear landing area in the garden. Dangling by my outstretched arms meant I only had about three feet to fall. As soon as I was over, I followed the garden wall until I reached to back of the garden gate. Besides the Yale lock there were two securing bolts, which, luckily, weren't padlocked. I drew back the bolts and turned the latch to unlock the Yale lock and held the door ajar, about half an inch. Within seconds, Max came through and I closed the gate behind her, leaving the bolts drawn back to save time later on.

"Did anyone see you?" I whispered.

"I wouldn't be here if they had." Max was looking all serious and surveying the busy garden, "We need to find a suitable hiding place, where we can see the back door." She lead the way and we found a hide behind the wooden sided compost shelter. We settled down with our helmets on the ground and rucksacks strapped to our backs.

"What time do you think Eve will get here?"

"Knowing Eve, she'll want to take her time, get everything set up. Then what does she always do before a shift at The Friary?"

"I've no idea? Go to the toilet?"

"Don't be daft. No, she stands outside having a smoke."

"God yer! You're right!" Come to think of it, I'd not seen Max smoking since the Punk Party at Cockerham Hall. " Not seen you with a fag in your hand for a while, have you stopped?"

"Yes, I thought it was only fair on you as you don't. Would you like some chocolate?" Max produced a bar of Dairy Milk from her jacket pocket and snapped it in two. I put a couple of chunks in my mouth and we both sat down with our backs to the heavy, wooden boards. It was a charming garden; lots of old, established fruit bushes which were beginning to fruit and ripen, blackcurrants, red currents and blackberries too. The garden was almost completely hidden from the neighbouring houses, so the chances of anyone spotting us racing across the lawn were practically zero. It was so peaceful sitting here and listening to the morning birdsong. Blackbirds were scurrying low across the lawn, arguing over the first worm.

"I forgot to ask you, is your Mum at home Max?"

"No, I sort of suggested she should stop at Gerald's for the night. They were going out for a meal, I changed my mind at the last minute, knowing Mum would react angrily towards me; I wasn't surprised when she rang later to say she was staying out the night. She's always trying to include me whenever they're out together. It would be easier on her conscience if I was there too, she wouldn't feel half as guilty for leaving me at home by myself.

"Don't you like him?"

"God no, he's so boring!" I was about to ask why when Max said "Shush Byrney, we ought to be silent from now on!" Max could sense my nerves were making me chatty.

The next hour went by slowly. We were sat huddled together as the morning dew and mist had caused the temperature to feel much cooler than we'd become accustomed to over the past seven or eight weeks of summer. Then we heard a noise inside the house. It was Eve. She had slid open the kitchen sash window slightly. She began dramatically flailing her arm about and shooing away something that had been caught behind the window. I had to bite my lip to avoid laughing. We could hear the kettle boiling too.

"Okay watch out!" whispered Max and she handed me a stocking from her rucksack. "Just put this on top of your head for now."

"You haven't got a gun in there have you?" remembering my dream.

"No why?"

"Nothing," I replied.

Max was issuing more instructions. "When we get to the backdoor, leave your helmet on the doorstep, okay?" I raised my hand to signal 'Okay'. After, what seemed like a long, dragged out twenty minutes later, we could hear the latches being drawn back on the back door and Eve appeared on the doorstep, puffing away on her bamboo cigarette holder. She was looking a little distracted, examining her watch and following the puffs of smoke she was producing as they ascended and dispersed. She pulled the cigarette out of her holder and dropped it onto a flagstone and stubbed it out under her shoe. As soon as her back was turned, Max grabbed my jacket pulling me to my feet and we raced across the garden, like commandoes exiting a helicopter. We pulled our stockings down over our faces, my heart was inside my mouth, pounding with every step. Eve had only managed to reach just inside the kitchen, when she heard us coming through the back door. Max was first in and when we came face to face with her, she crumbled to the floor, spilling her cup of tea. Max just caught her, moments before her head hit the ceramic floor tiles. We turned Eve over onto her back and left her lying there. Max was stood astride of her torso. She looked at me and said, "She's fainted. Quick, hand me the rope!"

"What rope?" I said "You were supposed to bring the rope!"

Max was thinking fast "Well go and find something in the shop to tie her hands and feet with." I dashed into the shop and found myself behind the counter. I could see the safe was open and my eyes just about popped out of my head; it was stuffed with piles of bank notes all banded together in neat wads. I tore away my gaze and leapt over the counter and began to examine the shop shelves for something suitable. It was all mainly stationary: exercise books, envelopes, pens, pencils; eventually, grabbing the only thing I could find, a wide roll of Celotape. I jumped back over the counter and into the back room to find Max. I held up the roll of Celotape so that Max could see what I'd found. Then tried to find the end of the roll. It was impossible with my gloves on so I took them off and wedged them inside my pockets. Max began to move about in an agitated way, "What are you doing?" she demanded.

"I'm trying to find the end of the roll." I found myself beginning to giggle which was only making it worse and Max more angry.

"Oh give it to me!" she said, already removing her gloves. I could see she was working from the wrong end of the roll.

"You've gone past it!"

"Where?"

"Back there!" Max was starting to join in with the giggling and it was in danger of getting out of hand.

"Here," I said, taking the roll and managing to get my thumbnail under the end of the tape and pulling out a good length. Max held Eve's ankles together and lifted then up, whilst I wrapped the tape around several times then cutting the roll free, by using my teeth to bite through the tape. We did the same to her wrists and I made sure Eve's head was comfy, by placing a towel under it from out of the kitchen. Max was already behind the counter, crouched down next to the safe and packing wads of bank notes into her rucksack. When it was full, I handed mine to her as well. At the bottom of the safe, were half a dozen wads of brand new, twenty pound notes. They looked very tempting, but Max said we'd better not touch them as they could easily be traced through their serial numbers. "Okay ready? That's the lot." She said. We checked the counter was tidy and moved into the back room. Max was about to make her way out when I said,

"Wait, Max! I just want to check Eve is still breathing. I lifted my stocking to get a clearer view. I put my fingers to her neck to check her pulse.

"Come on Byrney!"

"Just a sec." I turned back, to face Eve and I could have sworn I'd just seen her close her eyes, but I couldn't have could I? Eve's pulse was fine. At the rear door, we checked each other over. Max brushed away a few traces of moss from my legs, from my earlier climb up the wall. We removed our stockings and squeezed them in the top of our rucksacks, slung them over our shoulders, picked up our helmets and moved up to the garden gate. We eased the latch and slowly opened it a fraction, to listen for any noise on the other side of the wall.

"Better put our helmets on just in case," whispered Max. We stepped onto the pavement and quietly pulled the gate to, until the latched clicked back into the keep. We'd only taken a few paces when we almost crashed into a pair of ladders, heading towards us at eyeball height. The foot of the first ladder just skimmed the top of my helmet. I pushed Max into the road as there, blocking our path, were the two window cleaners.

'Bloody Hell!' I thought. They stopped and looked straight at us. Max and I were dressed almost exactly the same; we were the same height too so I suppose, in their eyes, we could have passed for brothers. We had obviously startled them as much as they had us. It was a strange meeting. After a long pause, we held our nerve and walked slowly past them as they continued up into the village. My adrenalin was pumping hard through my body. My legs were beginning to feel like lead. Max could sense my pace slowing and she moved in close. Our helmets bumped together. Rounding the slight bend in the path we could see the opening, only fifty yards ahead. I was saying to myself, 'Come on! Take the money and run'. Once we were through the gap, we raced into action. My Fizzie was still tucked into the side of the hedge. I began to feel more relieved. All we had to do now was to find somewhere out of the way, to park up and remove the Fizzie's disguise. We daren't head back towards the village now, so our only option was back down Hook Lane, towards the railway bridge. I took my rucksack off and crammed it into my top box but it was so bulky I couldn't reclose the lid. Never mind it'll have to stay like that. I jumped on and kicked the engine into life. Max threaded herself in behind me. We rode past her house, under the bridge and as we rounded the corner I braked to a halt.

"What wrong?" asked Max

"I came this way earlier this morning and I didn't see anywhere to hide between here and the Main Road. On the public footpath, down by the river, I remember seeing an old stone building, in the distance on the other side?"

"You mean the old weavers mill?"

"Yes, probably, is there a way across the river to get to it?"

"Only the clapper bridge, but I'm not sure it's strong enough."

"Let's give it a go - the path looked deserted just now." I turned my Moped around and headed back to the railway bridge. To the right of the bridge, next to the stile, was a farm gate. Max jumped off and opened the gate. Once I was clear, she closed it again. We employed the same procedure at the next boundary, on the far side of the field. We carried on following the river, past the bend in the path that lead up to the Recreation Ground. We were making our own path now, towards the next boundary, about two hundred yards up ahead. We could see the old mill across the river, but the clapper bridge was on the other side of the hawthorn field boundary and there was no gated gap for us to ride through. The hedge ran down the slope of the riverbank and just before the water's edge, there looked to be just enough room for the Moped to squeeze through. There was just one problem, how to get down to it. The bank was very steep and the narrow, rough ground next to the river had several exposed rocks. It would normally have been beneath three feet of water, but the summer drought had taken effect. The ground had since been churned up by cattle too - some of their old hoof prints looked quite deep, but at least they were dry. I asked Max to get off and walk down to the gap while I straightened up the Moped, in line with the slope. The edge of the field was about ten feet above the height of the river and was slightly overhanging the edge of slope too. If I wasn't careful, I could go 'arse over tit' to coin another of Dad's favourite expressions, or worse still, severely damage my Moped. Max was looking up at me "Get on with it, but be careful!" I edged my front wheel over the precipice, with my right foot holding on the rear brake. The soil broke away, nearly lurching the handlebars out of my hands. I quickly released the brake the Moped descended almost perpendicular and dug into the ground as it levelled out, almost unseating me and throwing me over the handle bars. No serious damage done, I don't think and checked the top box to make sure my rucksack hadn't fallen out. Max helped me pull my Moped around and we wheeled it in and out of the potholes, scraping the pedals against the exposed rocks. Then, by snaking the handlebars from side to side we managed to sneak through the gap, without falling into the water.

The clapper bridge was a much trickier obstacle. It was made up of two long slabs of granite, about four or five inches thick and each one must have weighed ten times more than my Moped. Max walked across it first. "Easy-peasy," she said smiling and waving me on. Her smile was the only encouragement I needed. There were no handrails and no curb to hang onto and it wasn't wide enough for me to walk alongside my Moped, so I started the engine and aligned the front wheel with the centre of the first slab. I noticed the slab was leaning over to one side. 'This should be interesting, watch out Evel Knievel!' It had to be done in one continuous movement - a bit like passing my Moped test all over again, except that this time, just one mistake through overbalancing, would be catastrophic. I concentrated on the bridge about three foot in front of my wheel and went for it. Max had forgotten to mention the step down at the other side and as the Fizzie bounced off it, I put a dent in the exhaust silencer. Could've been worse! I looked up ahead at the approach to old stone mill. It was mostly an undisturbed jungle of nettles and briars. I parked up and we went to find the entrance together. There was an old cart track, leading away from the mill and up and out of sight over the ridge.

"Do you know where this goes Max?" I said, pointing at the overgrown tracks.

"Yes, it leads into Weavers Lane, you must have passed it this morning along the Main Road." Perfect I thought.

The mill was a single story sandstone building, with windows along the south facing wall only. We found the rusty iron door in the gable end, slightly ajar. Its iron hinges were seized solid but, by our joint efforts of forcing the door and kicking away a few clumps of turf, it was just possible to increase the gap wide enough for us to pass through. There was one central room inside. Parked up at the opposite end was some ancient, rusty iron framed, farm machine with huge rusty, iron rimmed, spoked wheels. There was loose straw scattered everywhere about, which looked like the dregs of last years' harvest. The four, iron framed windows were still intact but covered in a thick layer of dust and cobwebs which made it impossible to view through them, but they let in enough sunlight to flood one half of the room. Beneath each one, the wooden sills had been robbed out and the plaster below had fallen away, revealing the bare, random stonework. The inside of the dusty old building had me intrigued. "What do you think went on in here?" I said, turning to face Max again.

"Can't you guess, I did say we are at the end of Weavers Lane."

"Looking at all this straw that's lying around, I thought this might've been a scarecrow factory."

"Very funny, but aren't we supposed to be doing something?"

"I'll go and get my Moped" Max took off her helmet and began to peel off the sticky back plastic. When she heard me approaching the iron door, she began to pushing from her side. I put my Moped on its stand and pulled the door from my side too. Together, we gained another twelve inches in the gap and after ten more minutes, we were stood looking at my Moped, its original livery restored with the original number back in place too. Rearranging the contents of my top box I managed to get the lid locked back down with my rucksack inside. I'd not been able to resist putting my hand inside to touch the wads of cash, just to confirm it was actually real. Max threw her rucksack to the ground and breathed a deep sigh of relief. I looked at her and couldn't contain my excitement any longer and blurted out "We did it! We fucking did it!"

"How do you feel?" said Max, smiling.

"Like Bonny and Clyde, like Billy Joe and Bobbie Sue" I shouted.

"Shush not so loud. Come here I've something important to ask you?" Max grabbed the waistband of my coat and stepped backwards into the sunlight against the white powdery wall taking me with her. She stared into my eyes and said "I want a baby…now!"

"I'd like to volunteer," I said smiling and looking around at our rustic surroundings. She pulled us both down to our knees and continued to look deeply at me, the sun highlighting her long lashes and dark freckles gliding down both sides of her nose.

"I'm serious, I want a baby." She took of her jacket and laid it on top of the straw. Then she began unbuttoning her jeans and kicking off her trainers, with the toe of each shoe pressing against her heels. "Come on, take off your clothes," she said smiling. I stood up and my eyes widened as she removed her socks and underwear and lay on her coat. She was completely naked. Her breasts fell flat beside her arms. Her nipples were like brown, upturned, Denby saucers. She reminded me of some photos I'd seen in the school library, inside an encyclopaedia about old African tribes. Max was such an exotic creature. I take a mental photo of her and store it away in my memory forever. I couldn't get my clothes of fast enough. Max began to giggle. After what seemed like too long to me, I was lying on top of her. I could feel Max's warm breath on my cheek and the sun on my back and Max's hands behind my waist. I'd had this dream many times before, in the final moments of sleep. The rays of the early morning sun were glittering through the gaps of narrow trunks of trees that lined the horizon. As the sun poured through to me, a dark shape flashed across each golden shaft of light. A big friendly bear was thumping hard against the ground, as it moved towards me in a gentle charge, getting faster and closer, until he grabbed hold of me, lifting me up. I closed my eyes and with my face in the warm sun, he squeezed me harder and harder, spinning me round and when he'd had enough, he let me drop. Max's hand tightened against my back and I heard her breath become shallow and delicious. We lay locked together in our own absorbing aura. Then, abruptly, I was brought back down to earth by something absurdly licking my leg. I looked over my shoulder to see a Jack Russel dog, at the end of a lead. The other end of the lead was attached to the hand of a startled looking pensioner. I let out an angry cry and moved my leg away sharply to shake off the dog, at which point, Max sprang to her feet and stood rigidly, shouting at the intruder.

"Well have you seen enough you old pervert? Take your dog away and fuck off!" The old letch went red in the face, pulled at the lead and marched away quickly.

"Max, for god's sake put some clothes on," I said laughing. I'd already got my jeans buckled up.

"Bloody pervert, staring at us like that." What's happening to Max? I thought, she was turning into a hooligan.

"Calm down, he's gone now."

"Well really, he was bloody enjoying himself." We dressed together and I pushed my bike outside. The old letch and his dog were nowhere to be seen. Max put her rucksack over her back and carried both our helmets as I pushed my Moped and we walked along the overgrown track together, towards the distant ridge.

"That was your first time wasn't it?" asked Max

"Okay, don't rub it in, there has to be a first time. I'm so glad it was you." As the track began to rise, I stopped and said I would have to ride my Moped from here. We kissed passionately, like two young lovers do, then Max handed me her rucksack. I slung it over my shoulder and kicked the engine into life. We agreed to meet up later. Max walked away, directly into the sun, back down past the mill and over the clapper bridge. As she disappeared out of sight, my emotions were doing somersaults. I pulled on my helmet and rode off up towards Weavers Lane and the Main Road.

I was glad to see the contoured, white panels of our caravan, as I rode over the speed ramps and the last few yards towards home. I wheeled my Moped around to the back and parked up so that the concrete slabs behind the shed were shielded from view. I'd fixed the slabs so that they could be lifted up. Beneath, was a thin sheet of plywood, which I'd cut to cover the sunken, ammo box that was now set into the hole. My vinyl forty-fives, which had been stored inside the ammo box were now in scattered piles, beneath my bed. I opened the ammo box and placed the stolen number plate in the bottom. I figured I would lose it later on. Then I took the cash out of each rucksack and wrapped it inside plastic carrier bags, to keep it dry. I was pleased with the result, as the cash just fit snuggly inside. I thought about counting it, but reckoned it would take too long and besides it would be more fun if we counted it together. I shut the lid, replaced the plywood cover and the concrete slabs. Next, I replaced the fence posts and bags of sands that had been there from the beginning. I stood back and checked it over. Everything blended in together, like it had lain untouched for ages. I put Max's rucksack back in my top box and stored mine back under my bed. It still wasn't quite Midday, time for a coffee and maybe a drop of something to steady my nerves. Christ! What an unforgettable morning.

I met up with Max by the swings at Crowston. I'd walked it all the way, to give me time to think. I stuck to the public footpaths across the fields, which was just as well since I'd spotted two Panda Cars zooming up and down Gunford Lane. I was trying to relax but I was more concerned about Eve than about being arrested. According to Max, she was resting at home, none the worse for her ordeal. I consoled myself to the thought that we'd been kind to her during the robbery. Had it been some other thugs stealing the cash then she could have come out of it much worse, even killed.

"Mum came home earlier this afternoon, it only took her five minutes before she had a rant at me." complained Max.

"Do you want me to go round and sort her out." I said, sounding all brave. I had been hoping Max would've greeted me with a kiss, or called me darling, or something.

"I think you've done enough sorting out for one day," she said, and then leant across, gently kissing me on the lips. "You were quite amazing."

"I thought we made a great team, Max and Byrney!" I handed Max her rucksack and she opened it.

"Oh nice one!" reaching inside, she found the two cans of Guinness that my Dad had bought in for me whilst they were away. We opened them together. Not surprising, they burst open, spraying us both in froth.

We lazed about for a couple of hours, on the swings and the merry-go-round, talking, making plans and getting our cover story worked out, in case the worst happened. I felt I was taking the lead in the conversation. Max had moved on, for her the robbery was done and dusted. I was thinking about us in the old mill. Neither of us had discussed the possibility of her discovering she was pregnant at a later date. For me, it seemed a little bit unlikely, for Max I could feel it ran much deeper, like an obsession that could not be ignored. Finally I said, "My folks are still away if you'd like to come back to my place and don't mind slumming it for one night?" Max was staring down at her trainers, making patterns in the dry sandy soil. Her legs were nicely bronzed and looked amazingly powerful too. Was it Private Fraser from Dad's Army who'd said? "I like strong thighs in a lassie!" Max could probably have outrun me easily, if we were ever chased by the law.

"Okay, why not! As long as you don't snore?"

"Only when I take my teeth out," I teased, pulling a face at her with my lips drawn tight and opening my mouth so that it looked devoid of teeth. Max pushed me over and we walked away, leaving the swings tied together as our signature trademark.

Max jumped on my back and we wobbled down the footpath in the silent, endless sunshine. We walked further along, side by side, feeling as tired as the old river. Max was beginning to feel down again too, saying how ugly the world was becoming. "There's so much hatred and anger; it's right there in your face, every time you turn on the TV news: Innocent people and animals being abused, or shot and blown up."

I said "Have you ever wondered what happens to our words after they've been spoken?"

"What? You mean like they have a life of their own or something?" Max sounded unconvinced and slightly cynical.

"Well, sort of. Actually, imagine all these words that we say to one another are floating around on invisible sound waves. Some, special words, like love, are filtered out by the trees and stick to their leaves; the trees collect them all year and finally in autumn, they turn golden. The more times people use the word love, the more golden the leaves become. Look at those sycamore leaves there." I pointed at a tree at the bottom of one of the gardens on Green Lane. "They're turning golden right now, I love you."

"Put a sock in it, you're making the cow's milk cuddle." And right on cue, we heard a cow mooing in the distance. "See!"

The closer we got to my mobile home, I was thinking of excuses for it being so small and how it takes a bit of getting used to. I was more relieved though, not to see Mum's car parked up in front. It would be just my luck that they'd decided to return home from their holiday a couple of days early. As we walked up the path to my main door, I said, "Would you like to see where the money's hidden?"

"No thanks, the least I know the better. Actually I'm not sure if I ought to stay the night here. I don't want my Mum wondering where I am and phoning the Police or something stupid."

"Do you want to come in for a coffee or something?" I tried not to sound disappointed.

"Sure, do you have a phone?"

"Yes, in the lounge. It's one of those Trim-phones like they used to have on the Golden Shot."

"You make the coffee and I'll call a cab. Shall we say one hour?" Max winked at me.

"Okay, let's skip the coffee."

Chapter 11

When The Rains Came

The next morning, after the post had been and there was still no letter from school, I rang the school secretary as Fionn had suggested. I was told not to worry and to come to school the following morning, between ten thirty and eleven. I don't suppose it mattered to me whether I'd passed or failed. The idea of joining the RAF was now dead in the water. It was easy for me to think that way, sat here by myself. No doubt once Mum and Dad were back, they'd be pushing me into a career of some sorts. The reason I'd wanted to join the RAF in the first place was because I saw it as an opportunity to travel and see more of the world. The alternative was going to college and university and I wasn't remotely interested in more schooling. I'd walked away from all that. Besides my feelings for Max were now taking the driving seat. My plan now was to find our little island, make lots of babies and drink Guinness.

The next day, I was feeling my familiar nervousness again pulling into the school entrance and parking my Moped in the staff carpark. I had a good look round at the complex of modern buildings, which housed all the academic classrooms. One or two memories instantly came flooding back. Like when Mike Lowry smashed the Chemistry Lab window, one break-time. Normally, when we played football in the schoolyard, it was the ball itself that was in constant danger of causing damage. Not in Lowry's case. He'd taken a shot at goal and his right shoe had flown off straight through the large glass pane. On another occasion, on the slippery path up to the Maths building, he'd accidentally set fire to his school trousers. Being one of the smokers, he always carried a box of matches about him. On that fateful day, they'd been inside his trouser back pocket. He slipped and fell on the gravel and, as luck would have it, the matchbox burst into flames. After Mike had been treated for mild burns in the first aid room, his sorry tale quickly circulated around school. After this, Geoff Garrity always called him 'Fireball'. When the following Physics lesson was over and the class room emptied, Geoff being the kind of generous bloke he was, gave Mike a disposable lighter.

Once through the main door, I ran up the steps towards the staff offices on the upper floor. Next to old Beaver Face's office was Miss Pringle, the school secretary. She was working alone, doing her admin.

"Hello Byrne," she said, "I have your results written down for you. Your certificate will be posted out by the examination board at a later date. Good News! Six passes. Three A's and three B's. Well done, a lot of students this year have been disappointed." She handed me the piece of headed notepaper and wished me all the best for the future. I was well chuffed as I leapt down the steps; all my hard work had paid off. As I was walking back to my Moped, I saw a girl and her Mum walking into school. It was 'teacher's pet', Belinda Hunt. She looked glum and red in the face, when I told her my results. She'd already been in earlier that morning and was back again with her Mum to make sure the school secretary had written down her grades correctly as they were all C's. I was laughing to myself, as I pulled on my helmet and rode out of school for the last time, revving the engine and pulling a wheelie.

Friday morning, I suddenly remembered Mum had asked me to pay the papers, leaving me the money for it on the mantle-piece. They were coming home later so I walked across to the corner of Grant Road to the Newsagent and while I was in there, he asked me when Anthony would be back from his holidays, whether it was Sunday or Monday? I thought I'd give Anthony a longer break so told the newsagent it would be Monday evening when he'd be back doing his paper round.

The Courier headline on the sandwich board read, 'LOCAL POST OFFICE RAIDED'. I bought a copy and began reading it, walking back home with a renewed flush of fear. Further into the story, it said that the Police were looking for two men with Liverpool accents according to their star witness, Mrs Herbert. Also, two window cleaners had come forward and given the Police the registration number and a description of the getaway bike and... shit! What was this? The Police were able to recover a fingerprint from a length of sticky tape that had been used to bind Mrs Herbert's hands. Bollocks! I can't believe it! How could I have been so careless? And by the way, the estimated size of the haul was twenty-two thousand pounds in used bank notes. I felt hollow and light headed and looked around, thinking I was about to be arrested there and then. I rushed home and thought I'd call Max on the phone, even though we agreed not to. Max's Mum answered the phone with a "Oh it's you!" she said, in her disdainful way. Max came to the phone and said she'd read the paper, that I shouldn't panic and that we'd talk about it tomorrow at work. Easy for her to say, I thought. It was my fingerprint the Police have under their microscope.

I looked out of the window and 'stone me', as I did so there was an old, forgotten sound of tapping on the roof of our mobile home. It was actually raining, incredible! I opened the main door and danced around in the garden with my tongue out, catching a few tasty drops, just as Mum, Dad and our Anthony arrived back in their car. Dad was cursing as he opened the boot lid and began carrying suitcases into the porch.

"Don't just stand there like cheese at fourpence, give me a hand with these bags!" Anthony shot past, wearing a green tartan hat. Mum had the kettle on already.

"Go and get a dry t-shirt on, you'll catch your death."

"It's only a bit of warm water."

"Don't argue and come and tell us what's been happening whilst we've been away." She handed a towel to me, and cups of coffee to everyone else.

I told everyone about the good news with my exam results, which won me a kiss on the cheek from Mum, a pat on the back from Dad, and a shout of "Good one, Bruv" from Anthony who was busy emptying his new sea shell collection on his bed, sand and all.

"Well they'll have to take you now in the RAF, won't they!" said Mum to everyone present.

"Aye, you'll be doing your square bashing before you know it."

"Take no notice of your father, he only wishes he was twenty five years younger." Dad didn't answer. He had picked up The Courier and was skimming across the headlines.

"I see some lucky bugger's got away with twenty-two grand from the Post Office in Crowston. Sez here it's a pair of Scousers."

"Crowston! You weren't caught up in it, were you?" Mum said, looking shocked but obviously thinking I might have been an innocent bystander. Trying not to look alarmed at her question, I played it down.

"No, happened early morning, before I'd even started work." I'd no idea why I said that, as I wasn't at work that day.

"Well, that's a relief, they might've had guns."

"Sez here, they tied up the shop keeper with Celotape."

"Well that sounds a queer going on, how stupid. They sound like a right pair of amateurs."

"No love. They were Scousers."

"Well if the Police know so much already, they'll soon have them caught. I wouldn't want my shop raided in broad daylight."

I was desperate to change the subject. "How was your holiday then?"

"Oh you would have loved it! The weather was glorious all week. Your father had a great time of course, singing songs with all the locals in the bar. Even Anthony went swimming in the sea." Blimey, that must be a first, I thought. He normally hides behind a deckchair under a towel. Then Dad got up and ran outside to close Anthony's car window, which was letting in the rain. He flew back in and said,

"Well I think this calls for a celebration. How about I pop out for fish and chips and a few tins from the off-licence? Still on Colt 45, or is it Guinness now?"

"Colt 45 please Dad"

"And don't go anywhere near that pub!" Mum shouted after him.

For once, we had a family evening in together, watching re-runs of 'The Saint' on TV. Even Dad looked to be enjoying a night in too, slouched in his easy chair, absorbed with the local news and complaining about the rain already. I was the least relaxed, feeling jitterish every time a pair of car headlights drove in front of the lounge window, thinking it was the Police coming to arrest me.

"Think I'll have an early night, work in the morning"

"Aye, good night lad." Said Dad, looking up from his paper.

It felt like a while since I'd last done a shift at The Friary, having been at home all week. I decided against mentioning to Max about the jittery state of my mind. It was the usual Saturday crew and we were all busy sweeping the carpet and laying the tables, as usual first thing. Next to the large table, where we usually ate our lunch, I noticed there were some new coffee table books for sale, on the shelves with the other gift shop merchandise. I put down my brush and flicked through a glossy book of Seventies Rock Stars. A section of photo's caught my eye. It was Paul McCartney and his wife Linda and their young children, living together in a shack somewhere in Scotland, with sheep, lambs, horses and dogs. The scenery looked wonderfully wild and remote and it looked like they were all having lots of undisturbed, peaceful fun. I called Max over.

"Look at these photos. This is what we want isn't it? Imagine raising our children somewhere like this?"

"Are you sure?"

"Yes, they'd be no one to bother us."

"No, I meant are you sure *you* want it Byrney?"

"Yes, with you by my side, I would. Do you think we've enough money to buy a place like this?"

"We could buy a Castle at least with our little hoard," said Max smiling.

The kitchen door swung open and Madge appeared. We recommenced brooming.

"Byrney! Edward has a little job for you this morning, in the house."

"See you later," I said to Max, doing my best 'looking enthusiastic' expression "Think about it?" It looked like Max might take a little convincing, but I was confident it was a great plan and fit in perfectly with Max's idea for raising children, with love and beauty all around, away from the ugliness in the world. I was so excited I wanted to leave right away, but first I'd better go and see what Edward wants me for?

It turned out it was the usual humping and dumping. Edward took me through to the house, up the stairs to the top landing where Kevin was already waiting, at the foot of a ladder leading up to the open hatch into the loft and looking slightly pissed off. This looks ominous I said to myself.

"Hey up Kev, you're in early."

"Byrney-"

"Right lads," said Edward, rubbing his hands, "One of you needs to go up into the loft and pass down everything that's lying on the floor - there's only a few boxes and some other things. I've got a lamp rigged up so you'll be able to see what you're doing. Right, who wants to go up first?" Kev was a couple of inches taller than me so, as I was the shortest, I volunteered.

"I'll go." I climbed the ladder and looked up at the state of the underside of the roof. There were tiny chinks of light coming through the gaps between the old stone slates, but worse, still, the loft was filthy with thick black dust, not to mention thick black cobwebs, hanging down from the rafters, too.

"Start passing it down to Kevin and I'll take it into the spare bedroom," instructed Edward. "And Byrney, whatever you do, only walk on the joists." I took it to mean the two-inch wide wooden beams and not the thin wattles of wood that held the plaster together. Some of the boxes would only just fit through the hatch and it was a real struggle to keep my balance and manoeuvre around at the same time. When we cleared the last box of old paperwork, I needed to get back down onto the landing as the air beneath the slates was swirling with black dust. When I was standing upright again, Edward handed me a glass of water and Kevin burst out laughing.

"What's wrong?"

"You should see the state of your face Byrney."

Edward had disappeared and returned five minutes later pushing some large rolls, wrapped in clear polythene, up the staircase.

"Have you ever used this stuff before?" enquired Edward, looking at the pair of us. We shook our heads. "Loft insulation," crowed Edward "Try not to let it touch your bare skin, otherwise it might be a bit itchy for while afterwards. Here, put these gloves on. Right, you'll both have to go up this time. Start from the end wall and roll the insulation out between the joists, it's made to measure." I climbed the ladder first, followed by Kevin. After twenty minutes of Edward passing up the rolls, we'd almost finished. "How are you getting on lads?" Edwards head appeared through the hatch door.

"One more roll should do it." I said as my foot slipped off the joist and straight, up to my knee, through the plaster.

"Never mind, never mind," said Edward holding out a helping hand. "Can you pull your leg out?" I did, to the sound of more plaster breaking, which went tumbling into the room below. The hole that I had made in the ceiling was directly over Madge and Edwards bed and was now covered in black dust and lumps of broken plaster. "Just leave it lads. I'll tidy it up before Madge sees it. You'd both better get back to the kitchen."

"Look at the state of you" said Fionn, when she caught sight of me.

"Don't ask! It's a good job Edward doesn't need his chimneys sweeping, otherwise he'd have probably sent me up there too."

"You look like you have already"

I went into the Gents toilet, grabbing a clean smock from the linen cupboard as I passed. Kevin was already in the Gents, looking fairly presentable and smoking a fag by the open window.

"Blimey, look at the state of you Byrney."

"I'm itching like mad too, what horrible stuff, glad that's over."

Then Kev started laughing, "should have seen Edwards face when your foot went through the ceiling. Madge is going to kill him when she finds out."

"Serves him bloody well right!"

When we both returned to the kitchen, I thought Madge was joking when she told me to go and wait on in the café as usual. What would the customers think? And also, come to think of it, why was Fionn in at work today too?

Fionn must have read my thought. "Sorry Byrney; Max has gone home, she was in tears earlier" She also must have seen the look of horror on my face. "Don't worry, it's just a girl thing."

"What is?" I was still looking puzzled.

"Her time of the month," said Fionn mouthing the words.

"Oh yes course" was all I managed to say. Shit! I thought. So Max isn't pregnant after all. I was OK with it as it meant we could go on trying, but I knew she would be devastated, she deeply wanted to have a baby. I was relieved when the end of the shift came around. I was tired and dirty and in desperate need of a shower. I'd pedalled into work again earlier in the day too, as I was still nervous about being seen on my Moped. (I'd let my Moped tyre down on purpose, in case Mum or Dad started asking awkward questions about why I was cycling to work). I really need to go and see Max but when Edward offered to put my bike in the back of his car and run me home, I hadn't the energy to refuse.

Nothing much ever happened on a Sunday in September. Dad was outside, washing off bits of Scotland from Mum's car. I was trying to think of reasons why girls broke up with their boyfriends. I'd probably had my fair share of disastrous relationships with girls my age at school. A few months ago, Jayne Collins from the mushroom farm on Green Lane, whom I was really taken with at the time, dumped me for the manager of our local supermarket, where she worked on the cheese counter. Okay, so her new boyfriend was a few years older than me, had his own car, good looking, wore a suit; steady well paid job too, I imagine - can't see what she saw in him. Maybe I *was* a bit backward at coming forward, or maybe I was a bit boring, I'd be the last to know. But I knew Max wanted me and I was determined not to lose her. I would literally follow her to the ends of the earth. I just wanted to make sure she was okay and the best way to do that was to go and see her face to face. I was moping around at the back of the shed when Dad found me. When he began to speak it made me jump.

"Oh! Here you are! I've fixed your puncture on your front tyre." He pointed at my Moped. "It only needed pumping up a bit. You'll have to keep checking it though, with a tyre gauge. You can borrow mind. I've put about twenty six psi in it."

"Thanks Dad." I said, forcing a smile. I'd no excuse not to use it again now.

"I'll take it out for a run then, make sure it's alright."

"Well don't be late for your Mum's Sunday dinner?"

I pushed my Moped past Mum's soapy car, kicked the engine into life and set off, looking through my handlebar mirrors to see Dad inquisitively watching me until I disappeared. Although it wasn't raining, the road was still wet from the downpour the night before. Sunday drivers were out in force and I was forced to bide my time, caught up in the plumes of water spray from their rear tyres. Summer was definitely over. Ever since we'd stolen the money I could sense the storm clouds gathering, like an executioners axe. I was glad to turn down into Hook Lane, taking the back way into Crowston. The road surface felt greasy and I was having to put my foot down around every bend, to help keep my balance. I parked up in front of Max's Mum's car and rang her door bell. Typically, Max's Mum answered the door. She didn't look pleased to see it was me. I suppose I did look a bit like a drowned rat. She had a cruel shaped mouth, slightly crooked, but beyond that she was dressed immaculately, in a classy Jackie Onassis style, not a hair out of place.

"Is Max in?" I could see she was annoyed at just having to talk to me. She looked the type who always liked to be in charge and sixteen year old boys were a push over for her.

"Maxine doesn't have time for the likes of you!" she said, attempting to close the door.

I put my hand up against it "Why not? I don't understand. Don't you like me or something?"

"Get away from my door." She moved away from me like I had some strange, contagious disease. "Frankly, you're the sort of distraction she doesn't need at the moment. Besides, she goes back to University next weekend and no, I don't like you and don't bother to come here again, good-bye." As the gap in the door began to close, I shouted into the hallway

"I love you Max!" and stepped back from the door as it slammed shut. I looked up at Max's bedroom window, hoping to catch a glimpse of her. There was nothing to see. I wouldn't have put it past her Mum to drug her, or something. She was a real, snotty pain in the arse. I'll just have to wait for Max to get in touch, I thought. Maybe she was just asleep after all, feeling a little under the weather. I guess I'd find out soon enough.

Thursday I'd been rota'd into the Friary covering for one of the permanent members of staff who was away on holiday. It was quite a different atmosphere in the kitchen. Madge was much more laid back. It obviously suited her, working with more mature staff. These senior members of The Friary crew only worked part-time through the week, handing out 'Afternoons Teas' to an equally older clientele. Most of them were married and lived in the village. One of the middle-aged ladies I was working with was called Ingrid. During our afternoon tea break in the café - it wasn't so busy that we had to take tea in the Madge and Edward's lounge - she was asking me about what my ambitions were. When I mentioned the RAF, she began talking about the war. Her accent was quite unfamiliar to me and she told me she'd been born in the Netherlands. During the war, she'd heard the RAF bombers fly over in the night and during the day and as a young girl, she'd found it very frightening. Her family became refugees, when fighting between the advancing Allied army and the retreating Germans had practically destroyed her town. It's remarkable to think that anyone alive today over the age of forty must have lived through the war and for many it had meant enduring the most life changing ordeals.

I was washing the dishes by the kitchen sink, looking out at the village square through the narrow gap between the shop and the café. I noticed an ambulance pull up near the gift shop door, with its siren going. Joanie, who was stood next to me, was standing on tiptoes and looking over my shoulder.

"That's strange, I wonder where they're going," she said and went striding off into the café and I presume into the gift shop and out through the entrance door. About an hour later, the ambulance departed, with siren and blue lights glaring away. Joanie came back into the kitchen looking flustered.

"Its Mrs Herbert, they've taken her to hospital." There was a loud gasp from the ladies in the kitchen and I felt the colour fade from my body, like a bowl of water being poured down the drain, as the guilt stung my conscience. This is bad, I thought, very bad. Joanie continued looking at Madge "I don't think she'll be coming back again."

"What do you mean exactly?" said Madge looking shocked

"That nice young doctor from the Surgery was with her and he told me afterwards she'd been diagnosed with Cancer, six months ago." It was the first time I'd seen Madge speechless. She just stood there with her mouth open, stirring a wooden spoon around in a frying pan. "There's worse." Joanie continued to tell us that Eve had refused to have any treatment. I couldn't comprehend what I was hearing. I had a feeling her health was worse than she was letting on - we all did - but nothing as bad as this. Well that's it! I thought. I'm definitely going to have to go down to Max's as soon as I've finished my shift.

Madge let me go at 5.00pm. It hadn't been a busy day and she said it was pointless having to pay me to stand around. But as I grabbed my jacket, Madge said that her and Edward had been talking as to whether I would like to work part-time, three days per week plus my usual Saturday. I didn't need to think about it. "Yes, I'd love to." At least it would get Mum and Dad off my case until Max and I had got our plans worked out.

I was stood over my Moped, which was parked in the usual place, when I noticed a Police car parked on the opposite side of the square in front of the Newsagent. Perhaps it's something to do with Eve's ambulance earlier. I didn't fancy driving past it on my Moped, so I decided, instead, to walk down Hook Lane to Max's house. From the opposite side of the square, I noticed the Policeman was stood inside the shop, talking to a group of women. The discussion was getting heated and I heard one of the women say, something like 'Aren't you going to call for help?' Help? Help with what I wondered. I rounded the corner by the Post Office. Strangely, there were a lot more people than usual out an about, on Hook Lane too. Some were knocking on doors and looking inside gardens. Further along, a buxom woman stopped me. She was puffing away on a fag and blocking the pavement. Perspiration was running down from the fringe of her sixties beehive. She wore a skirt that was too short for her age and her bare legs were mounted on a pair of wooden soled Scholl's. I thought she looked like the personification of 'Chuffing Nora'. A thick plume of smoke escaped from her moving mouth, as she asked me, 'had I seen a baby in a pram?'

"No, sorry." So this is what the fuss was about. The woman looked dejected. "I hope you find it." I said sympathetically.

She blew out her cheeks and let out a defeated sigh and turned away, allowing me to pass. She called across to her friend on the other side. "Any luck?" The other woman just shrugged her shoulders and they met up to in the middle of the road to have more words.

When I reached Max's house, I was glad to see the little blue MG sports car absent in the driveway. I rang the doorbell and Max opened the door, slightly to begin with, until she saw my smiling face.

"Hi it's me!" I tried to sound normal, but I could tell something was wrong. Her hair was flat and her eyes were red, like she'd been crying and she was acting evasive. Then, as soon as I spotted the empty pram in the hallway, I realised why. "Max, what the fucks going on?"

"Don't be angry Byrney. I couldn't help myself." She moved quickly into the lounge and sat down on her sofa, next to a sleeping baby, wrapped in a pale blue blanket. I couldn't believe my eyes.

"Max you have to take it back right now, this isn't right. I've just passed loads of people out there looking for it."

"No I want to keep it! please Byrney, we can go away somewhere today, all three of us." Max picked up the baby and cradled it close to her body. "It's a little boy, she said, he's so lovely" and she rocked it gently from side to side, looking into his eyes. He was still sound asleep.

I was beginning to panic. "Max don't be stupid, how can we? Please put him back in his pram, he's not yours. There's a distraught women in the Newsagent, at this moment, crying out in pain."

"Well she shouldn't have abandoned him outside in the street then."

"Max you're being irrational. Stealing money is one thing, but this is a little life. Max, please give him to me." I leant across Max and gently eased the baby out of Max's arms and the baby woke and instantly began to cry.

"See! He doesn't want to go back with you!" Max was scowling and her hands were locked, like they were about to strike. I turned away and settled the screaming baby back down in his pram.

"Someone is going to be knocking on your door any minute, I'm surprised the whole village can't hear him." I turned the pram to face the door.

Max moved across the room to block my exit. "If you take him away I'll never speak to you again."

"Please, get out of the way Max before we both end up in serious trouble. I understand how you're feeling, believe me."

"You don't know anything!"

"Max please!" I pushed her away and opened the door and pushed the pram out into the driveway. I could her Max screaming. It sounded much worse than I'd heard earlier from the baby's real mother inside the Newsagent. I was pushing the baby up the path as fast as I dared go, at least his screams had subsided. If I could just get as far as the open gap in the field then, maybe, I could make out I'd found him behind the hedge, where I'd hidden my Moped over a week ago. The further I went along Hook Lane the more certain I was of bumping into the women who were out searching for this lost child. Incredibly, I was almost at the top of Hook Lane, when a youngish woman saw me and rushed over.

"I've just found him," I said, feeling genuinely relieved for the baby and Max.

"Thank god, thank god. This way - follow me," she said. I was hoping she'd take the pram from me as we walked quickly around the corner, but no. "We've found him!" she shouted into the square at no one in particular and then the Policeman stepped out from inside the Newsagent, closely followed by the baby's Mum, who was now hurtling towards me and grabbed the baby into her arms, kissing his forehead with a sigh of relief, which quickly changed to an anger, and was aimed directly at me. At that point precisely, the Policeman arrived beside us.

"Well done lad," he said inauspiciously. "And where did you find it?"

"He was half way down Hook Lane," I said, looking behind me and pointing. The youngish woman next to me interrupted us. "We've already looked down there, two or three times and we never saw the baby!" and then she tried to hold onto my arm, but I pulled it away as the policeman reached into his breast pocket and removed his notebook, licked the nib of his pencil and looked down at me.

"You said *he* was half way down Hook Lane, tell me, how do you know the baby is a boy?"

Oh god, I was desperately trying to think of something to say, how do I get out of this one? "It's just a slip of the tongue, I didn't know he was a boy, I just said 'he' instead of it."

"Where exactly then was the pram when you found it?"

"There's a gap on the left hand side half way down Hook Lane, *the baby* was just behind the hedge."

"Did you ladies check there?" the Policeman asked, looking at the youngish woman who was by now lost for an answer too. Then, out of the corner of my eye I saw Joanie heading across the square from the Friary shop, to my rescue hopefully. The Policeman saw her too striding over towards us and began stretching out his chin, like he was preparing for a showdown.

"What's going on Byrney?" I was so happy to see Joanie's kind, friendly face.

"Do you know this young man?" asked the Policeman

"Yes, he works for me and he's only just finished work a quarter of an hour ago too, so whatever you're planning to do with him, you better get your facts straight first. Come on Byrney! It's time you got off home." The Policeman was left standing and looking on helplessly as Joanie linked my arm with hers and we strode back across the square. He couldn't see that I was beaming from ear to ear.

"So you've met our Constable Brown, or Constable Clown as he's known to everyone in the village," she smiled, "Don't worry about him, he's hopeless. If you put him in a round room and told him to stand in a corner, he wouldn't have a clue." Then Joanie looked lingeringly back across the square "At least that young girl got her baby back. Do you know, there's always one drama or other happening in Crowston. You get used to it. All's well that ends well."

"Thanks Joanie, I'll see you Saturday."

I was mightily relieved to be climbing aboard my Moped and setting off back home. That was a close call, too close for comfort. I was fast becoming a nervous wreck. The afternoon was still swirling around in my head, like one of Madge's minestrone soups - a melee of confusion. What was happening to my dream girl and our plans together? No matter which way I looked at what had occurred, I couldn't understand Max's behaviour, what was it that she couldn't tell me? I'd not even had chance to tell her about Eve either, or maybe Max already knew. Maybe that was when Max had taken the baby, in the distraction of the ambulance arriving, taking Eve away - to die in hospital. Poor Eve too, there she lay; her incredible life was almost over. If Max had been well, we could at least have gone to the hospital together and said goodbye to our friend.

Saturday morning, Madge had us all waiting in the kitchen until everyone had arrived. We were stood quietly, buttoning up our smocks and looking around at one another. Normally in these uneasy situations, no matter what awaited me, I always imagined something for worse. This time I was wrong.

"Some of you might know that Mrs Herbert was rushed to hospital two days ago. Well I'm afraid I have some more sad news. Mrs Herbert passed away earlier this morning." It was shock to all of us. Fionn, who was stood next to me began to cry and rushed out to the back room, closely followed by Vicky. "The funeral is likely to be this coming Friday and we've decided to close the Café that day, as a mark of respect. Anyone wishing to come along with us to the funeral is more than welcome to do so. We may even hold a wake for her afterwards too."

"Yes we'll let everyone know what the arrangements are," said Joanie glancing around at us in a caring way. "We'll also be sending some flowers too, from everyone here."

I wasn't surprised to see that Max was absent. Yesterday, I'd ridden to her house to find it in complete darkness and the driveway empty too. I'd anticipated not being allowed to speak to her, so I'd written a note to Max and placed it in a sealed envelope. I explained my feelings towards her. How I didn't blame her at all for what had happened the day before, how we can get through this thing together and I begged her to get in touch with me. Her absence at work today also confirmed to me that her Mum had finally had her own way with packing Max off to University. Later in the day, Joanie confirmed what I already knew. She told me Max's Mum had been into the shop yesterday to explain that Max had gone back down South. I held back my emotions long enough for my feelings to go unnoticed.

All in all, it was a very sombre day at The Friary; even the afternoon rush in the café couldn't dispel our sadness. Fionn and Vicky recovered their composure though, winning admiration from both Madge and Joanie as they worked the whole day with their usual thoroughness and warm spirits. About thirty minutes before knocking off time, Madge took me into the lounge to explain my new working hours. I was to get a slight pay rise too, but also I'd have to pay some income tax, but I'd still be better off. So on top of my usual Saturday, I'd now be working three afternoons a week, for five hours per day.

Outside Kevin was waiting for me. For once, I'd agreed to go for drink with him after work, at The Star. "Why not?" I'd said. So Kevin, Vicky, Fionn and me all piled into his little green Mini. Kevin and Vicky were huddled together as thick as thieves, having a private conversation, laughing and smiling at one another. Kevin had his arm over Vicky's shoulder. I hadn't even noticed they'd become an item. They both looked very happy. It started me off thinking about my relationship with Max and how her Mum had done her utmost to prise us apart. Hopefully it would all backfire on her one day soon. Max was very much her own boss and not the kind of girl that's easily lead. I took a gulp of my beer and turned to Fionn "How long have Kev and Vicky been going out together?"

"Ever since Kev started working at The Friary."

"They suit one another."

"What are your plans Byrney, still joining the RAF?"

"I doubt it!" Fionn looked surprised. "I haven't heard anything from them and besides things have changed over the summer."

"You mean Max?"

"Yes, kind of." I had a sudden impulse to confide to Fionn what had happened the other day in Crowston; she was the one person, I felt I could talk to, but I couldn't betray Max's vulnerability. I wasn't even sure it would've solved anything if I had. "You've known Max longer than I have, what do you think of her?"

Fionn looked puzzled "Why are you asking me? Surely you know her better, now, than I do."

"You're right. I was just a bit shocked to find out she'd gone back to Uni without telling me."

"Don't worry Byrney, Max isn't the type of girl to play around."

"Yer you're right." That was reassuring to hear from Fionn. "What about you Fi? Going to start College this month with everyone else?"

"Don't be daft! I was never any good at school. No, I'd like to go travelling, maybe France, or Spain. I could do a lot worse than working in a bar or a restaurant, perhaps even own a bar of my own one day."

"Yer, I can see you doing that. You'd make a great hostess. Somewhere sunny eh?" Looking at Fionn, my thoughts were distracted from my heart felt agony, from Max's absence, to somewhere sunny... "You should go for it Fi," I agreed.

There was an empty pint glass being waved in front of my nose. "Your round!" said Kevin.

"Same again, everyone?"

It turned out to be a wicked night at The Star. There was a live music from a Country and Western band and to say it wasn't really my sort of music, I enjoyed it more than I admitted to. By nine o' clock, the pub was heaving. We were stood in the glare of the lights, watching couples holler and yelp as they danced in a line, in front of the band. I'd completely lost count of how many drinks we'd had. We all made a fool of ourselves on the dance floor, not that we cared a hoot. It felt great to forget about everything else that had been happening recently. Kev and Vicky ended up sharing a taxi and I cadged a lift with Fionn when her Mum arrived to run her back home to Cayburn.

When I staggered into our caravan, Mum and Dad were furious with me. Why hadn't I phoned to let them know what I was doing? Staying out half the night! And where had I left my Moped?

'Fair point', I thought as my bedroom ceiling began its familiar pattern of rotation. I had to rush to the toilet to hooey-up, I could feel another lecture from Mum coming on. I woke up at nine o'clock the following morning, to the mother of all headaches. Fortunately it was lashing it down outside so at least I was saved from one of Mum's punishing hangover 'serves you right' jobs in her garden. Instead I was sat at the kitchen table, helping Anthony with his maths homework. He was having difficulty doing his long multiplication, using his logarithms tables. It wasn't easy teaching Anthony, he was usually in a world of his own at the best of times.

"Where's your log book?"

"Haven't got one!"

I found his logarithms book hiding in front of him and tapped him on the head with it. "What's this then! Okay, let's have a look. Your first sum is five hundred and twelve multiplied by one hundred and twenty-eight."

Anthony was back in La La Land, "Captains log, star date five one two, one two eight."

"Do you want to learn or not?" I was about to get cross with him, when I heard the phone ringing in the lounge, Mum picked it up.

"It's for you," she said, stretching the phone wire and holding it through the lounge door.

"Max?" Mum nodded in agreement. I couldn't get round the table fast enough, dragging a chair over the Lino and making the sort of noise that grated Mums ears.

"Hi, Max?"

"Hi Byrney, how are you?"

"Fine!" I could feel my heart pounding. "Where are you, what's happening, I mean how are you?"

"I'm sorry for the way I ran out on you but I'm coming back home again. I'm finished with University."

"That's fantastic, well you know, if you're okay with that?"

"I'm wasting my time here Byrney. It's not what I want anymore."

"What do you want Max?" I was hoping her answer included being with me.

"We can talk about that, when I get back. I should be home this Thursday night."

"It's Eve's funeral on Friday, why don't we go together?" Then I remembered that maybe Max still didn't know about Eve, "Sorry I didn't have chance to tell you, did you know Eve had died?"

"Yes, Mum told me." So, she had known after all.

"So you're okay really?"

"Yes, of course."

I could detect some hesitation in her voice and I thought it wise not to push her. "I'll call round for you then, on Friday morning?"

"Yes okay"

I looked round to see if Anthony was out of earshot, "Hey Max? I love you."

"I love you too Byrney." And she hung up. I punched the air then went and explained to Mum about Eve's funeral on Friday, that the café was closed all day and not to make any meals for me. She was pleased for letting her know.

"Now you're learning, it's not that difficult is it." last word to Mum!

Chapter 12

The Longest Day

Working my new part-time hours with the older members of staff had me feeling almost grown up. I never pretended I knew everything and they all treated me as they did each other, very politely and generous with their village gossip. The exception was Glenda. She could talk the hind legs of a donkey as Dad often said about his dear wife. Once Glenda had got her momentum up, there was no stopping her. Even Madge had to ask her a few times to check inside the café, winking at me, once Glenda was out of sight as peace returned to the kitchen. Whenever I was in conversation with them I was constantly feeling ashamed that I was hiding my dirty secret. My anxiety was once again detectable on the Richter Scale and I was back to peeping through the lounge curtains, when we watched TV in the evenings, checking every pair of car headlights that passed by, in case it was the Police. I think Mum was beginning to get suspicious of me too. She had a sixth sense for being able to read my thoughts. I couldn't sit there any longer. I had to retreat to my bedroom to count the money in my jar and read the local news.

The Post Office Story had now been moved to page five in The Courier. The latest was the Police were pursuing some promising new leads, but no details were mentioned. The manager and manageress of the Post Office had installed additional new security. And the pensioners and parents of Crowston had now all been paid their allowances, all be it a week late, but at least they were all happy again.

When the day of Eve's funeral began, I was sat at home in the kitchen having breakfast with Dad. The smell of bacon was doing wonders for my well-being. I was feeling good about seeing Max again. Just a few more weeks more and we'd be miles away from here. I'd bought a map of Scotland and was planning on taking several days to get there. Eve had once suggested I should take Max on holiday. It would do her a power of good, now more than ever. Dear Eve, god bless her! I couldn't help thinking she'd somehow played a part in the robbery. What was it Max had said? Eve let it slip about how much money there was in the safe. Very un-Eve like I thought and as we were making our escape, I could have sworn she was watching us as she lay unconscious on the floor. And where had that information come from about the Liverpool accents?

"How many slices would you like, son?" said Dad holding the grill pan over my plate.

"Three please, chef." Dad poured some baked beans over the bacon and added a poached egg each too for good measure.

"How are they treating you at that Café of yours?"

"Yer, fine. They seem to have more respect for me these days."

"Good" Dad shovelled in a mouthful and continued to talk. "Who's this old woman then, whose funeral you're going to?"

"She's called, was called, Eve Herbert. She worked for the French Resistance in the war."

"Get away!"

"Yer, she was married to a French bloke and they used to hide airmen in their basement."

"Sounds a bit hairy. She must have had a plenty of guts."

"Yer, fire in her veins too." I thought of her death and her husbands too. All those years apart and now they'd be together again. Was that possible? "Do you believe in life after death?"

"Not really son. Once you're gone, you're gone. Doesn't matter how powerful or rich you are, we all end up the same road.

Take that Howard Hughes fella who died a few weeks ago. Richest man in the world he was. He died just like anyone else."

I knew Dad was right. But I wanted to believe in something.

"Enjoy life while you can son, make the most of it - it's all there is and take my advice, don't get married." He laughed, revealing his half eaten food sticking to his teeth.

We were still having the same conversation in his little old van as we headed towards Crowston. "What's a Wake, Dad?"

"They're reight good do's they are. The Irish prop the coffin up ag'in a wall with t'lid off and all mourners walk round supping beer and chucking some of it over t'coffin."

"I don't think it'll be that sort of a do, today."

Dad was laughing "No I don't suppose it will lad. Whereabouts do you want dropping off?"

"Anywhere in the Square's fine." Dad pulled up outside the Newsagent and I got out and stuck my head back inside the van, holding the door open. "Cheers Dad. I'll probably be home late."

"Okay. Where's that black tie I lent you?"

"In my pocket." I said, tapping the side of my leather jacket.

"Okay lad, have one for me." And off he disappeared, spluttering back down the road in a haze of black smoke.

I walked down the now, familiar narrow pavement towards Max's house. It was a typical, breezy, Autumn day. The roads and gutters were full of dead leaves and debris. The oak tree overhanging the garden wall of the Post Office had been severely pruned back. The top of the wall looked a long way up. Even the gap into the field had a new aluminium gate fixed to it. In the distance I could see the path by the side of the river, it was unrecognisable from the summer. To my relief, Max's driveway was empty and my shoes crunched their way towards the front door. It opened, before I reached the first step. Max was standing in the open doorway, with a glass of red wine in her hand. She put her free arm around me, spilling wine from her glass onto the marble step as she leant forward.

"Oops!" She said and gave me a kiss. She tasted very fruity. She looked a little fruity too.

"Are we celebrating?" I said, wondering what was going to happen next.

****

Around the same time, Madge was just going through a few last minute instructions with her father-in-law Joe, who was looking after his two grandchildren for the day. They were all sat in the warm lounge. Janie and Joey had a game of snakes and ladders already set up and were patiently waiting for their Mum to leave them so they could start their game.

"Help yourself to as much tea and coffee as you like. Reenie is in the shop all day, I'm sure she'll have time to brew up for you." And turning to face her babies, "Right you two! Give your Mum a kiss goodbye." The two excited children duly obliged. "And behave yourselves for Grandad, no cheating and do as he says," she winked at Joe and paused to take in the happy fireside scene as young Joey began shaking the dice.

Joanie was just finishing off in the shop as Madge walked through from the house.

"Come on Joanie we have to be leaving in ten minutes."

"I've just had that good looking student boy in, you kno-"

"The one who drives around the village without a licence?"

"Yes him, he's just bought all the cheddar cheese, almost 5lb."

"Well you know why that is? It's so he can concentrate on his studies, or whatever else they get up to in that cottage, without having to bother to go to the toilet." Madge was cackling at her own joke.

149

"I'll just grab my coat and changed my shoes" and Joanie scuttled off into the dark, narrow hallway between the shop and the house.

"Have you seen Edward?"

"I think he's still in the kitchen." replied Joanie.

Madge stepped down into the kitchen as Edward was just cramming half a sandwich past his lips. "Nearly ready my sweet," he said, "won't be a minute."

Madge had other ideas. "Look at the state of you. For heaven's sake go and get a shave Ned quickly. We have to leave in less than ten minutes. And where is everyone?"

"I've told them all to wait outside."

Kevin's Mini was parked up next to Edward's new car. He was stood next to the driver's door, smoking a cigarette and talking to his fellow occupants, Vicky, Fionn and Frances. Five more staff were waiting there too, forming a circle to shelter from the gusts of drifting leaves. Chatterboxes Glenda and Julia were going with Edward and Tall Sue was taking the remainder of the group. Madge and Joanie stepped outside together and thanked everyone for coming. "Are we all here?"

"Byrney and Max haven't showed up yet," said Kevin as he flicked his cigarette stub into the empty road.

"Has anyone seen them?" The question was met with silent shakes of heads. "Well if they're not here in five minutes we'll have to go without them," said Madge, tut-tutting under her breath. Edward appeared from the shop, cleanly shaven and with a small piece of toilet roll, attached to a red spot of blood on his chin.

"Morning Everyone! Nice day for it," he said, as he habitually rubbed his hands together to warm them.

"We're just waiting of Max and Byrney" said Joanie

Edward looked round in disbelief. "It's not like them to be late." Tall Sue volunteered to stay behind and wait another ten minutes in case they turned up. The others drove off up the hill behind the square and past St. Mary's church. It began to rain as forecasted, a feeble drizzle to begin with and then as the wind gathered force, it brought on a deluge. Tall Sue waited longer than ten minutes. It was obvious no one else was coming, as the downpour had emptied the square of all forms of life. Her red Ford Escort coughed to life with the damp and headed up the hill in the wet tyre tracks of those who had gone before. The rain ran down in torrents at either side of the road, depositing leaves across the water grates leaving only a few gurgling gaps for the slurry to sink down into the drain. The village was slowly changing into an unfriendly, untidy mess. A large pool of water, big enough to drown a cat in, had formed at the lower end of the square. It covered the kerb stones and was threatening to enter the row of shops and cottages. Another storm was just a kiss away too.

****

"I've decided that while Mum's away in Toronto, I'm going to drink all her most expensive wine. Would you like some?" Max hiccupped and waddled off towards to kitchen.

I called after her, "Blimey Max! How much have you had?"

She returned with two full glasses "Only the one...bottle!"

Nothing was ever straight forward with Max. She wondered over to the stereo and placed an LP on the record deck. I recognised the tune instantly. "Beethoven?" I wondered if my little joke was lost on her. "So is it true? You've chucked in University?" Max moved up close and stared deeply into my eyes, like she was trying to connect to my soul. But, her eyes were glazed over; she didn't look like she was in the same room as me. I held onto her waist to stop her from overbalancing.

"Never do, what someone else wants for you. Otherwise you'll be at their beck and call forever. I never wanted to go to university in the first place, but it was *expected* of me. You must

151

go to Oxbridge la-di-dah-di-dah! I'll bet your Mum's not a cow like mine!" and Max slumped into an armchair still holding the bottle and glass upright.

I wanted to get Max away from having more to drink, so I turned the volume down on the stereo. "Listen Max, don't you think we ought to be getting ready for Eve's funeral? I really don't want to miss it. How about if I make us a coffee?" Max jumped to her feet and despite her behaviour, she still looked very cute in her pink t-shirt and white shorts, with her toes sinking into the fluffy rug.

"Why don't we go upstairs to my room instead?" she said smiling "I've missed you." I hesitated for a moment and that was all it took for Max to lose her temper.

"Am I not, good enough for you now?" Max was just managing to get her words out in the right order.

"Come on Max, you know I'm crazy about you. We've got the rest of our lives ahead of us. Please, let's just concentrate on saying farewell to Eve." Max walked over to the stereo and cranked the music up, louder than before. I followed her and turned the volume back down again which lead to us squabbling, at first, until it became more physical and we were tearing into one another. We were both evenly matched, wrestling over the damn volume control button. I managed to have one hand holding down the control and the other holding Max away at arm's length. She grabbed my hand and bit it hard.

"Christ Max! What's got into you?"

Max's eyes were wild "I've still not forgiven you for taking away my baby, that's what's got into me!" I couldn't take in what I was hearing. "If you're not going to stay with me, you can fuck off." Max retrieved her glass from the table and topped it up to the brim until it overflowed and ran down the stem.

"Don't be like this Max. I want to understand what you're going through. We can work it out together and we can have our baby, not someone else's. I want to have a child that reminds me of you, of us both.

"You *knew* how much I wanted a child, something pure and beautiful. You're not the person I thought you were."

"What about all the money we have? Was that all for nothing?" She wasn't listening.

"You're a let-down Byrney, no you're not, you're a fucking coward!" Max's words were starting to hurt. I looked around the lounge at the mess we'd made. I imagine her Mum wouldn't be too impressed. I began to tidy up a couple of cushions off the floor.

"Let's not argue Max." It sounded feeble, but I was trying to diffuse Max's anger.

"I want you to leave me alone"

"Please Max let's just talk sensibly.."

"I want you to go, now!" She was looking round for something and grabbed the empty bottle. "Leave, me, alone" She lifted the bottle, aiming it at my head.

I put my hands up to defend myself. "Okay I'm going but it's not the end Max. I'll come back tomorrow."

She lowered the bottle and screamed "Get out!"

I backed away towards the front door "Just remember all the great times we've had this summer and we can still have more like them." Somewhere in the back of her mind was a memory, a recognition, like she saw how wonderful it had once been between us. I sensed a tiny glimmer and took a step towards her. Perhaps she'd no fight left. Then, she looked up at me vaguely and spoke in a softer, defeated voice

"Just go. Say Goodbye to Eve for me."

"Are you sure you'll be Ok?"

"Yes, please just go." As I closed the door behind me, I heard the music start up again – Kashmir.

I ran all the way to the village square. There was not a soul around, not even a stray dog, not a dicky bird. There were a few sandbags at the door of the newsagent that was now closed for the day. The rain was bouncing off the tarmac and the cobblestones in front of The Friary. Even the old stone water trough was overflowing. I'd never seen so much rain water in the village. Behind Madge and Edwards house, I could see the clock tower at St. Mary's, against the darkening sky, I was over half an hour late. Somehow, I felt claustrophobic. I hated being late. I had no choice other than to run up the hill to the church to see if the funeral service was still in progress. The tall trees in the Vicarage garden were creaking and moaning, like the mast of a ship, caught in a storm. Leaves were falling like tears. My leather jacket clung to me like a second skin. I needed to get out of the rain quickly.

I reached for the heavy oak door and stepped inside the church, closing it firmly behind me. Drops of water were running down me and pooling at my feet. I wiped the rain from my forehead with the echoes of door latch still ringing out in the cool, silent air. I squinted my eyes into focus at a figure sat in the first row of the dark wooden pews. I wiped my eyes again and my heart jumped. It looked like Max, impossible I thought and as I moved down the aisle, to get a closer look, I saw it was actually a girl of about ten or twelve years of age. She looked round at me as I slowly walked towards her. She seemed strangely familiar in her yellow dress and scruffy dark hair.

"Hello!" she said, in a way like she was expecting me to be there.

"Hi, I'm looking for Eve's funeral? I thought it was taking place in here today?" Clearly I'd missed it. I moved round to the front to face the girl who was smiling and looking at her hand as it moved over the end of the pew.

"Look at all the beautiful things you can see? I like to just sit here and imagine the people who made them. Did you know they sometimes leave their marks somewhere out of sight, just a shape or a squiggle? You have to search for them, look!" And she moved her hand away from the end of the pew where it had been resting, to reveal a letter T, with a line like a snake twirling around it. "See what I mean?" she smiled. As we sat there she had me looking around the old church, too. My mind was elsewhere though. Inside the church the atmosphere felt safe and impregnable, but it wasn't helping me to say one last farewell to Eve.

"Sorry, I have to find my friends. Have you seen anyone here at all this morning?"

"No! But perhaps they're outside in the graveyard?" She stood up and held out her hand. "Come on, let's have a look together." She was a charming little creature and taking hold of her hand seemed like the most natural thing to do. I was shocked by how cold it was as she leaned backwards, levering me to my feet. "Follow me!" And she skipped off towards an arched side door that lead out into a stone vaulted porch way. My attention was caught by an old, brass, water tap, mounted in the wall. It was green with corrosion, looked like it hadn't been used in years. "Walk up the path and turn right. That's where the new graves are." The shiny, stone slabs lead away up through an iron gate. I was hoping I would see a huddle of figures, but the graveyard was motionless, except for the red and orange leaves that were still splashing over the gravestones. I turned around to thank the little girl, but she was gone.

I was feeling annoyed at myself, for not paying attention to the details of Eve's Funeral. All I had to do was turn up at The Friary at 11.00am and that was that, if only. The rain was easing back to a fine drizzle. I walked back down to the square and noticed Ingrid who was just leaving the VG store with a bag of shopping.

"Ingrid" I shouted as I ran over to catch up with her.

"Gosh, you're in a state." she said, "What have you been doing?"

"Getting wet mostly." I said, still feeling the drips running down the back of my neck. "Don't suppose you know where Eve's funeral is taking place? Think I've probably missed it now anyway."

"Yes, you probably have! She's being cremated over at Calderhouse. If I was you, at this time of day, I'd go straight to The Star. Madge mentioned to us all earlier in the week, there was going to be a little reception for her, around two p.m today." She tightened her headscarf and trudged off in the direction of Hook Lane. "See you!" I walked over to the Post Office, feeling inside my pockets for some loose change. Inside the telephone box, there were a couple of business cards for local Taxi cabs, wedged in the corner of the metal frame, where the Dialling Code Index was fixed above the phone. I resigned to waiting inside the call box until my taxi arrived, passing the minutes by studying the lifeless goings on through the rectangular, clear Perspex panes, that were branded with burns from fag ends. They never replace the broken glass panes in phone boxes with real glass anymore, do they?

I was glad to see the warm inviting lights from table lamps illuminating the front windows at The Star. Edward's car was in the car park and Kevin's green Mini with it's white roof, was there, too. Kevin was the first to spot me as I entered the function room at the back of the pub. He began to laugh "Bloody hell Byrney! Fell in the river or what?" I ignored him and sat down opposite him, next to Fionn.

"Where's Max?" she asked.

"She's not coming." I was still going to defend her, despite all she had said. Most of her words were still thumping around in my head. Maybe I was a coward. I was even beginning to doubt my own sanity.

"Is she still at University?"

"No, she came home last night but she's just changed her mind, that's all. Actually she had a few drinks." I decided to be honest with Fi. "I'm not sure she even wants to be with me anymore."

Fionn passed me her glass of wine. "I think you need this more than I do," she said quietly.

Joanie came over and asked what had happened to us both. I explained to her that I'd got the details mixed up and that Max had fallen out with me over it. When I arrived late at The Friary, I went straight up to St. Mary's instead.

"Never mind, you're here now. I'm sure Mrs Herbert would've appreciated it."

"There's a couple of French people here for the funeral too," said Fionn pointing with her eyebrows at a bald headed man standing next to a younger version of himself - presumably his son. "I think they might be distant relations."

Joanie provided the answer. "It's Mrs Herbert's brother-in-law Henri and his son. I always thought Mrs Herbert was a spinster. According to Henri she was married before the war." So that's Henri and he's come all the way from Nice too. I felt sorry for him knowing how much he once felt about Eve. He was immaculately dressed in a dark suit and looked like a decent sort of guy. I went to the bar and grabbed some sandwiches from the buffet. It had been a long time since I'd last eaten. I settled into my chair at Kev's table and listened to all the gossip. No one had an unkind word to say about Eve. Henri tapped his wine glass with a teaspoon to get our attention. He introduced himself and spoke about how he came to know Eve before and during the Second World War, in France. I could see the look of incredible surprise on most people's faces. Henri described some of Eve's experiences, how brave she had been and how she had been forced into making a huge sacrifice when she fled back to England alone. He finished by saying that all her friends were welcome to stay at his Hotel in Nice, if we ever found ourselves in the south of France. We all raised our glasses to salute Eve.

Madge came over to our table for a few words. "Joanie's been telling me what happened to you earlier, Byrney. I thought you had more sense. Walking round a graveyard when we were all at the Crematorium." I made a few more feeble excuses about not paying attention. "You've been working me too hard Madge." Luckily, she thought it was funny. It felt wrong to be making jokes at a funeral, but no one was going to arrest me for that. After we'd polished off the buffet and shifted out into the car park it had finally stopped raining for the day. My jacket was more or less dry, having spent an hour and a half on top of a radiator in the function room. Edward kindly offered to take a few of us home before returning to The Star to collect Madge and Joanie.

Fionn was studying one of the business cards which Henri had been handing out to everyone. "What do you think of Henri?"

"I liked him, seemed a very polite person, generous too." Fionn's first impressions of Henri had been exactly the same as mine. "Are you in work tomorrow?" she asked.

"Yer, supposed to be. That's if I haven't caught pneumonia." I joked again.

The couple of glasses of wine at Eve's wake had changed my mood for the better and I was beginning to imagine a happy ending to my troubles as I waved goodbye to Edward's car. It turned back up the Main Road and sped away after dropping me at the main entrance, but as I turned the corner towards my home I suddenly froze with fear. There was a police panda car parked outside our caravan and a uniformed policeman was talking to Mum. I was about to turn and run, but Mum spotted me, then the policeman turned around to face me and I thought, this is it, the game's up. I hoped it was me he'd come for and that Max was still in the clear. Mum began to talk to me as I moved within earshot of their conversation. "The policeman wants you to go with him to the Police Station for identity purposes. He also wants to know if you know someone called Maxine, what's her surname again?"

"Miss Maxine Reid" confirmed the policeman.

I must have gone as white as a sheet as Mum raised her fingers to her lips and said "Don't worry, it'll be alright." I'd no idea what story the policeman had spun to Mum but clearly she didn't suspect I was a masked robber. The policeman opened the passenger door and I reluctantly got inside. When he slammed his car door to and sat behind the wheel I was expecting him to slap a pair of handcuffs on me. I almost offered up my hands in anticipation. Instead, I decided to stay quiet until I discovered how much they knew. Inside the police station waiting area, I was 'checked in' at the desk then escorted, by the desk Sergeant, through a side door and down a corridor to the far end, where I was led into a room with a glass partition. There was no furniture, apart from a couple of white painted steel, built-in cupboards and a marble work surface, covered with some official looking forms, which were laid out in a row. So this must be where they beat confessions out of suspects then? I could imagine blood being swilled away and brushed down a plug hole that was hidden under a loose floor tile. A scruffy man, walked in wearing a crumpled brown suit. He looked like someone who had come to collect some lost property. Unfortunately for me, it was someone I would soon learn to be wary of. He was introduced, by the serious looking Sergeant, as one Inspector Derek Atkinson, CID. I could see he was holding a sealed envelope in his right hand.

"You're Mr Mark Byrne of 22 Bowland Mobile Home Park?"

"Yes" Here we go I thought. 'Under the terms of the Geneva Convention I'm only allowed to-

"I've a letter here with your name on it," he announced, holding up the pink envelope for me to see. "Have you ever seen

a dead body before?" I was stunned. They'd obviously got it wrong. It must be some other Mark Byrne who'd lost a dead body. Maybe I didn't hear him correctly.

"Sorry. A dead body, Why?" Had they dug up Mrs Herbert as part of some ghoulish piece of evidence; it didn't make any sense? There again, neither was I. Eve had been cremated.

"I'm sorry to have to inform you that a Miss Maxine Ried was found dead, two hours ago. Suicide. We'd had some complaints from her neighbours about loud music and when, eventually, we forced her door open, we found this letter in her hand, addressed to you. Unfortunately, we've been unable to contact her guardian."

This isn't really happening. "She's in Toronto," I Mumbled.

"Pardon lad?"

"Her Mum's in Toronto"

"So we gather. Now look, before we hand you this letter, we'd like you to take a look at her to identify her for our records." Atkinson was pointing at the glass screen. "She's lying in the next room." I stared at the glass and the shabby looking plastic curtain. I couldn't take in what they were saying. It had to be some kind of mistake. There was no way Max would take her own life. I could feel my legs shaking and I was trying hard to steady them as we walked round into the next room. Atkinson moved me into position, his hands on my shoulders. "Okay Sergeant." The Sergeant pulled back the white sheet covering her face. She was still wearing her pink t-shirt. There was no mistake. Even with no breath left inside her body, Max was absolutely, serenely beautiful. I placed my hand on her hair, I could still feel her power over me. I wanted to lie beside her, Max, wake up, wake up.

"Is this her?"

I turned to the Sergeant and nodded.

"Sorry lad, you have to say yes or no, for our records."

"Yes! This is Maxine Reid. Yes this is her, happy now?"

Atkinson released his grip on my shoulders "I gather you both work at The Friary, but your names weren't on our list of colleagues of Mrs Eve Herbert?"

"No, we didn't normally work with her." His question had caught me off guard. Although I could see immediately where this was leading. Just keep it brief Byrney, stay calm.

"You own a Moped too, I believe?"

"That's true" no point in denying it, I thought, "So do half my mates."

"It's just routine Byrne. Where were you on the morning of August 22nd?"

"When the Post Office was robbed in Crowston, you mean? I was with Max." This was also true. "We were out walking by the river." Also true. "Didn't see anything suspicious though, if that's what you'd like to know."

"We have to ask, in order to eliminate you from our enquiries. If you can just sign the formal identification paper," and Atkinson lifted his right arm towards me, offering me his pen. That was odd, his hand was gloved. I looked at the paper on the marble work surface, coolly placed my hand inside my jacket pocket and pulled out my work pen,

"It's okay, I have my own." and quickly signed the form without bothering to read it. Atkinson and the Sergeant looked at each other like they didn't know what to do next.

Atkinson stepped forward and picked up the forms and began rolling them up, "Thank you Byrne." He turned to his Sergeant. "Go and ask WPC Alexander to take young Byrne home."

"It's okay, I'll see myself out." I said, holding out my hand for Max's letter.

"Yes of course. Thank you for coming this evening." I took the envelope from his hand and marched out the door and down the corridor.

I didn't know it at the time, though I should have suspected. Atkinson was too wily a character to let it drop at that. He'd spent years staying one step ahead of the opposition. Even, if it meant beating up the wrong guy, in order, to have his way. The cogs inside his brain rotated and when they'd aligned themselves together, it spelt trouble. My leaving the police station wasn't the end of the case at all, not as far as the police concerned:

Atkinson was still stood inside the last room, squeezing the rolled up pieces of paperwork and planning his next move.

"Do you think he was one of the men who robbed the Post Office?" asked the Sergeant.

"If I did, he wouldn't have left here. Love and hate would have seen to that." Atkinson demonstrated his technique by thumping his fists together. "My gut feeling tells me Byrne is still hiding something."

"But Byrne doesn't have a Scouse accent!"

"Mmm, quite." Atkinson was rubbing his chin, not entirely convinced how reliable that piece of information was. "What's the latest about that stolen number plate?"

"We've been in touch with Southport CID and they're now saying that Benson couldn't be one hundred percent sure that his number plate was on his motorbike that morning he rode up to Cockerham Sands.

"Really?"

"Apparently, he reverses his motorbike down his garden path at the side of his house so that it's easier for him to ride out when he next uses it."

"Bloody Hell! So that just leaves us with a dodgy witness statement from a woman who's now dead and an unknown fingerprint on a piece of Celotape. Looks like we'll have to hope new evidence comes to light bloody soon, before the trail goes cold."

"Right boss"

Atkinson wasn't impressed with the progress that was being made so he let some of his frustration fly off at the ineffective desk Sergeant. "And the next time we have someone like Byrne into the office, make sure you bring a parent along or we'll be laughed out of court for not following correct police procedure." Atkinson slammed the rolled up forms into the Sergeant's overhanging belly and moved towards the exit. As he pulled down the door handle he looked over his shoulder and as an afterthought said "Just one more thing." The Sergeant prepared himself for another blow to his authority "What was the name of the big guy with red hair, who you took over from when we both arrived here last year?"

The Sergeant looked puzzled "You mean Lofty?"

"Yes Lofty. Any idea what he's doing now?"

"He was talking about doing some private investigating, but who'd employ a thug like him?" The Sergeant said in disbelief.

"Do we still have a phone number for him? I've got a little outside job he might be interested in."

It was a clear, starry night outside the Police Station. I had Max's envelope in my hand and walked across the road to the park. Apart from a couple of dog walkers exercising their pets, I had the place to myself. I rested my right foot on a dewy, damp, bench seat and under the pale light from an old, cast iron lamp and stared at the front of the envelope.

BYRNEY

C/O THE FRIARY

I took a deep breath and ran a finger inside the envelope breaking open the top edge and pulled out Max's letter.

I'M TOO SCARED TO FACE THIS WORLD ANYMORE

YOU ARE THE ONE PURE INNOCENT PART OF MY
LIFE

I KNOW HOW MUCH YOU LOVE ME PLEASE DON'T
BREAK YOUR HEART OVER ME I'M NOT WORTH IT

IN TRUTH I DIED A LONG TIME AGO

REMEMBER ME ON THAT SUNNY DAY BY THE OLD
MILL

THATS WHAT I'M THINKING OF NOW AS I SLEEP

I SHOULD HAVE SAID THESE WORDS TO YOU
EVERYDAY

I LOVE YOU

TAKE MY DOLL I WANT YOU TO LOOK AFTER HER
SHE KNOWS ALL MY SECRETS

PLEASE FORGIVE ME

I read it three or four times, trying to get inside Max's thoughts
to understand why I'd not seen this coming. Max had been acting
strange for the past couple of weeks, but nothing to suggest it
would end like this. I folded her letter carefully back inside the
envelope and headed down the hill into town and at the first
phone box I found working, I called Lewis and asked him to meet
me at The Shepherds.

The pub was starting to fill up. I sat there twirling my pint
around on top of a beermat. It felt like I'd aged a hundred years
in a day. Every time my emotions began to quiver, I took another
sip of beer. The jukebox was playing a new song by Abba,

Dancing Queen. How can everyone else be so happy? I was wishing I hadn't come in for a drink, stood up to leave, when Lewis walked in and uncharacteristically, gave me a hug and patted me on the back. If anyone understood a little of how I was feeling, Lewis was the closest. He punched me lightly on the arm "I'll get em in." He returned with two pints and two whiskey chasers. Holding up the small tumbler towards me, he nodded. "Down in one." The sharp taste of alcohol brought me back into the room.

"Thanks for meeting me, mate"

Lewis raised his eyebrows and lifted his pint glass to his mouth. "Don't be daft, that's what mates are for." He waited for me to start talking, but I couldn't begin to find the words so I handed him Max's letter. When he'd finished reading it, he said no one had ever thought of *him* like that. "I really feel for yer, surprised you're not in a bigger mess."

"I just can't accept she's gone."

"Give it time Byrney, things have a way of sorting themselves out. When I went to Andy's funeral the other week, his Mum was in a terrible state. She could hardly walk by herself. There were more tears for her than there were for Andy. Times like that you find out who your real friends are." What Lewis was trying to say was that it's worse for the ones left behind. Yes, they had to deal with the grief of losing a loved one, but they shouldn't turn it into an unbearable burden that they must face alone. But, for me, there was more to it. Andy's Mum knew she would never have another son, just like I knew I would never find another Max. How can you live life faced with impossibilities? The answer is you can't. You can only do what *is* possible. It wasn't the reassuring answer I was searching for at this moment, but it was a start. As the crowd at the bar grew larger and louder I wanted to find somewhere quiet.

"Think I'll walk home, get some fresh air."

"Stay a bit longer and I'll give you a lift home. My Dad's picking me up at closing time."

"No it's okay thanks."

Lewis was reading my body language "What yer doing tomorrow?" he asked.

Tomorrow? Oh God, Saturday. There was no way I could face working all day at The Friary. "Erm nothing."

"I'll call for you in the morning. Let's go off somewhere for the day?"

"Why not."

Chapter 13

Road Trip

I drew back my bedroom curtain and stared at the Taylor's caravan next door. Their little white poodle was yapping away locked inside their glass porch. I could see his head, bouncing above the window sill. Last night, Mum and Dad had been very consoling and sympathetic. We talked to one another as a family and in the midst of that warm conversation I'd let my guard slip and was unable to hold back my tears, but having to listen to some of Dad's unkind comments, like, 'there's plenty more fish in the sea' meant, they soon dried up. He can be an insensitive sod at times. I was packing my school sports bag with a few spare clothes. I decided I needed to take my road trip, now more than ever. The jar in the bottom of my wardrobe had nearly one hundred and fifty pounds saved inside. That's more than enough. Moving outside to transfer the rest of my stuff into my top box, I also had a quick glance around the back of the shed to make sure nothing had been disturbed. Now that my hidden stash had an added covering of dead leaves, it looked more natural than ever.

Mum was on the phone to The Friary explaining I was taking a weeks holiday. In any case, I was almost certain I wouldn't be going back to work there again. She popped her head out of the main door to say it was okay to take time off, but they insisted I call in today, to see them.

"Just do as they say," she said. "It'll only take a minute. They just want to check you're okay, that's all." I really couldn't face them, but I'd no choice. I could here Lewis's Moped rounding the corner. His Suzuki had a very distinctive sound now that he'd removed the baffle from his exhaust silencer. If my Moped sounded like a hair dryer, Lewis's Suzuki sounded like someone blowing their nose. Mum was still insisting on having the last word, as always.

"Have you got everything? Soap? Toothpaste?"

"Yes Mum, can I get going?"

She passed me a folded ten pound note "Your Dad wanted you to have this. Please be careful on the roads, we'll be worrying about you."

"I'll be fine, see yer!"

"And don't forget to ring!"

I leant into Lewis's visor and said I'd a slight detour to make.

I walked into the VG shop at The Friary and the first person I saw was Joanie, who gave me a peck on the cheek. Even Madge gave me a one-armed hug. It was left for me to decide if I wanted to carry on working there. They all hoped I would. Fionn was stood in her smock talking to Lewis. She rushed over as I closed the shop door behind me. She put an arm across my shoulder, like we used to do at school.

"It's so awful about Max. There's been quite a few tears in the café this morning. I thought you two looked great together. What are your plans now? Will you be going to Max's funeral?" I knew I wouldn't be welcome there. And besides I much preferred to say goodbye to Max alone in my own way. My feelings were still very raw. Just hearing someone mention her name had my nerves tingling with despair.

"Don't think that's likely, Max's Mum hates my guts."

"Are you going to be coming back to work?"

"I'm not sure Fi. What about you? Still fancy owning your own bar?" I was trying not to sound miserable.

"That's my dream. You know what they say don't run before you can walk." She smiled at a new thought "It would be nice just to go abroad one day."

I admired her spirit. "Sounds like a great plan, Fi" I looked at Lewis who was fidgeting with his gloves. I could tell he wanted to get going.

"Promise me one thing Byrney, when you've made your mind up about your future, promise me you'll come back first and let me know."

I was beginning to feel choked up again. "Ok Fi, I promise." She smiled again; her mission accomplished. She turned and ran back inside the café.

"I'm bloody starving." moaned Lewis "Let's grab some breakfast at Firton Services."

"Good idea." We revved up our machines and sprayed the village high street with a trails of blue smoke. Some slight retribution at least for my soaking yesterday. For those who work at the Services and for a few others 'in the know' it was possible to access the Motorway Service Station via a back entrance, totally illegal of course. Even more so on a 49cc Moped, but it was usually fairly quiet on a Saturday morning and according to Lewis the traffic police don't work at weekends. Fifteen minutes after leaving Crowston we were sliding our trays along the cafeteria counter, bathed in plastic, Formica luxury. It was a soulless place to eat in comparison to The Friary. We were chomping away at our full English. I had one eye on my plate and one eye scanning through the New Musical Express that I'd just picked up from the newspaper kiosk.

"How long do you reckon it'd take us to get to Manchester?"

Lewis was mashing a sausage between his teeth as he spoke, sounded like 'bout four hours!'

In the week that followed, Max's letter was in my pocket the whole time and instead of just one day, Lewis decided to stay with me for the whole weekend too. After a long ride to Manchester, which included several, unscheduled stops - we'd both had different ideas on how to get there - the Saturday night gig was a revelation. It was held in a crumbling old building called The Last One Standing. The band I was really looking forward to discovering were called The Stranglers. The all wore black clothes and looked mean and ugly. In fact the whole city seemed full of ugly faces. The gig really rocked. The floor was bouncing; the lights were blinking; plaster was dropping of the walls and the music sounded raw and energised. By the end of the gig I'd completely changed my mind about punk rock sounding childish. The musicianship of The Stranglers was really impressive. They took it in turns to perform solos and it was like they were skilfully making it up as they went along. What left its mark on me too, was the reaction of the crowd. As the music played they jumped and kicked and crashed into one another. It was like being in The Kop End at Deepdale when Mickey Robinson had just buried the ball in the back of the net, terrific. It felt great to be part of this new tribal revolution.

We'd booked into a bed and breakfast for two nights. It wasn't exactly comfortable, but it was cheap and the food was okay, if you liked it drowned in lard. Sunday was a wash out - not that there was a lot happening anyway - but Lewis found a snooker club and we rented a table for a couple of hours. At least the locals were all friendly towards us too, after hearing our strong, Lancashire accents. The pub nearest our B&B was called The Criterion and was part clad in sickly green, coloured ceramic tiles, which had probably once been all the rage back in days gone by. We decided to make it our local for the weekend. The beer tasted like washing up water, but it didn't spoil our fun. We parted company after breakfast, on Monday morning. Lewis was heading back home. I was getting worried about whether he'd find his way back home okay as he kept saying he was going to stop off in Chester in his way back. "Don't you mean Chorley?" I kept saying. I watched his trail of blue smoke disappear then I set off in the opposite direction. I was heading up to Skipton, in North Yorkshire, to stay with my Uncle Ray as pre-arranged by Mum. It was one of the conditions she'd insisted upon, when she'd reluctantly, agreed, to let me come away. At least she knew where I'd be staying, for half the week. Mum's brother was a school teacher. 'He got all the brains' my Mum used to say and still does. The truth was, Mum had a lot of brains too, but she'd chickened out of going to Grammar School, preferring instead to go to a Secondary Modern to study fashion and home economics. I guess it paid off for her in the end.

Uncle Ray was your usual scratchy chalk and blackboard duster chucker, definitely old school. He wore leather elbow patches on all his sleeves and lived by himself in a pebble-dashed detached house about a mile out of town. I loved his untidiness. It had an organised structure to it, that only he knew about. Ask him to find a certain book and he could lay his hands on it almost immediately, despite the fact there were several tea chests full of them, still scattered around various rooms of his house in need of emptying. "I've been meaning to put up some shelves for almost twenty years." he joked. He liked to talk about the war a great deal, which was fine with me. His stories were mainly centred around helping my grandfather supply Anderson Shelters to homes around Yorkshire. Well, we can't all be heroes. After three days mooching around Skipton, where everyday appeared to be a market day I was getting ready to see what was over the next horizon. We said farewell and Uncle Ray packed me up the most delicious beef sandwiches I'd ever tasted. "Family secret" he said, tapping his long, Roman nose.

My next stop I'd discussed with Uncle Ray was to find the source of the River Wharfe, which ran through Skipton. "Good luck with that one!" he'd said. I was travelling up to Hawes and thought I'd take the old gated road up from Buckden.

I'd been up this particular road before, one Friday night just before last Christmas with Lewis and his older brother, Dave, who played the drums in a pub band called Jumping The Gun. It had been a pitch-black night and it'd felt like we'd been on the road for hours. Lewis and me had reckoned the only reason Dave allowed us to come along was to keep him company and help carry his kit. He owned a mini van and I'd drawn the short straw on the way up. I was crouched in the back, hanging on to the sides of the van around the twisty, bumpy, single track roads. The gig was being held in a village hall that appeared to be in the middle of nowhere, but was packed out with locals by the time the band cracked up to play their setlist of Queen covers.

Before the gig started, Lewis and me had strolled down to the one and only village pub. It was like stepping back in time. The landlord served up his brew in large, copper jugs that he filled directly from the barrel, which lay on a wooden cradle, at the back of the bar. The frothy beer tasted amazing. We had noticed at first, the pub had quite a spooky atmosphere. Every time the door latch rattled, the entire inhabitants of the pub all looked round to see who was entering their den, but by the second pint we'd felt right at home.

I was hoping to find this very same pub again today, on my way up to Hawes, but if it wasn't on my route, then at least I'd be able to admire the spectacular Dales scenery instead. I noticed the harsh landscape had begun to bare itself for winter as the sun slowly arced across the limestone hills. It was the perfect day for a ride out on my Fizzie. The gates slowed my progress, but I found the inconvenience of them great fun. The slippery cattle grids were a different kettle of fish until you got used to riding across them, upright and in a straight line. It felt like an endless journey. It was so absorbing, it was almost impossible to remember anything previous, as if in my whole life I'd just been travelling from one remote village to another. I was still following the course of the Wharfe and as I crossed it for the umpteenth time, there in front of me was the familiar white stone pub from a year ago, The George. I parked up at the front and lifted the latch ready to be stared at. Disappointingly, there was only one other person in the pub besides the landlord. He was obviously the local game-keeper, leaning against the bar, dressed in his deer stalker hat, plus fours and a shotgun by his side. I had a very enjoyable ploughman's lunch and was pleased to see the landlord still serving up the local brew in the traditional way, in jugs, straight from the barrel. Looking round at the roaring fire and the old oak settle, I was beginning to regret reserving my accommodation in Hawes as I would have loved to have stayed the night here in spite of running the risk I could well be offered up as some sort of human sacrifice.

The rest of my trip I found myself looking at desolate farmhouses and imagining I was Paul McCartney in a shack somewhere in Scotland. I even caught myself talking to Max about whether this or that was suitable for kids, dogs and horses. Her letter was still inside my breast pocket next to my heart, as it had been since that awful day. So far this week, I'd been avoiding making a very serious decision. I had to think about what I was going to do once I was back home in West Lancashire.

The landlady at my B&B in Hawes had said I'd not lived until I'd seen the view from the top of Ingleborough hill. It was on my way home and I could take in the Ribblehead viaduct too. It sounded great.

The walk around Ingleborough was around five miles and it didn't disappoint. Not surprisingly there was fresh breeze blowing, but the well worn path was well sign posted and easy to follow. As I climbed higher the panorama opened up all around. I could see for miles. I'd had a song in my head ever since I'd woke this morning. I was beginning to find the lyrics connecting me to Max inside the landscape;

The love I'd felt for her was all around, blowing and shining and like the scent of this freshly toiled earth, it surrounded my soul.

Standing on the summit I finally reached a decision about my future. I wasn't someone who enjoyed being lonely. I thought about my family and friends and everyone at the café, but it was time to move on and step out into the big wide world. I needed a quest, an obsession, a mystery, something to put right in the world and then it struck, right between the eyeballs. Once I'd reached my decision, I headed South West again, for the last time.

When I arrived back at our mobile home park it was three o'clock in the afternoon and I had the place to myself. On top of the TV in the lounge, there was a letter addressed to me from the Armed Forces Careers Information Office in Preston. I folded it in half and stuck it inside my jeans pocket. I dumped my gear in my bedroom and went outside to check behind the shed to make sure everything looked safely untouched. Then I headed back out across the lorry park and up Grant Road. I knocked on Fionn's door. Her Mum opened it with her usual friendly smile. "No it's okay I won't come in, thanks." I heard Fi's footsteps pounding down the stairs. "I've decided what to do with my life" I said "Thought you might like to be the first to know." Fionn's eyes lit up with shocked surprise.

Chapter 14

Departure

It was only a short walk from Preston Bus Station. The high street shops were just opening up. Some were having their floors swept, others were picking up the mail and turning around their 'Shop Open' signs. I continued down Fishergate, dodging piles of empty cardboard boxes and delivery drivers stepping across my path, until I reached the third shop from the end and paused outside. I stared at the large photo cards in the window of The Armed Forces Careers Information Office. The colour photos showed young members of her majesties forces do exciting jobs and exciting past-times too: driving a tank, working on an aero engine, water skiing; it all looked very tempting. I've been inside these offices a couple of times already this year and now I'd finally been accepted. Eve had been at pains to dissuade me from joining up and it was down to her now that I'd decided to take a few months out to think it through. Eve's story had deeply touched me and I still owed her for the part she'd obviously played in the robbery at the Post Office. She had done more than put the idea in Max's head, I was sure of it, and I was also convinced she'd made a false statement to the police too. I wouldn't have put it past her to have faked fainting, just to make it easier on Max and me. So as it was unlikely anyone would come forward to collect her ashes, I'd decided I would try and locate where her husband Paul had perished at the hands of the Gestapo during his attempt to get away from France more than thirty years ago and that, at a later date, I would reunite Eve's ashes with her husband Paul. I knew my chances of finding the exact spot were remote. Perhaps my search would be met with a wall of silence too, but it was a challenge I was unquestionably drawn to. This was now my mission.

Twenty five yards past the Armed Forces office was the ramp that lead down to the entrance of Preston Railway Station. On the wall of the pedestrian walkway was an old black and white cast iron sign 'Trains This Way' with a finger pointing the way. The glass sash window at the ticket office slid upwards, about thirty seconds after I'd rung the attendant's bell. I bought a single to London Euston and walked down to Platform Two, admiring the huge Victorian, cast iron columns that supported the spectacular lacework iron structure of the roof. The columns were decorated with roses around the uppermost stem. Overall, it was an immense structure, a cathedral to the architecture of travel. I loved the business of activity, men and boys in uniform pushing trolleys of mail, blowing whistles and the sound of the diesel engines revving up and dislodging the air until it rebounded from the glass canopy high above. I sat on a cold bench seat outside the waiting room. I took off my rucksack and rested it by my feet. Then, once again, I began observing the comings and goings along the platform. I put my hand down the inside pocket of my leather jacket to make sure my passport was still there. The photo was not one of my best. I'd had it done at the photo booth in Woolworths at Lancaster. I'd been wearing my crash helmet that day and my hair was flat to my skull like I'd just come out of the shower - not that it mattered really as this was my first passport and it was only valid for twelve months. However, the 4th October 1977 sounded a very long way away. I'd arrived early at the Station so that I could really enjoy the whole journey, without feeling tense. I was in bad need of a shake down. I looked at my reflection in the waiting room window. Wondering how I looked to the rest of the world.

It had been a hectic week leading up to this departure. I had to somehow conceal enough money about me without it looking suspicious or posing a risk of being robbed. Earlier in the week I'd been to see Kevin about doing some modifications to my new aluminium framed ex-military rucksack. He'd cut the horizontal and vertical tubes and fitted collars over the joints that were secured by two screws. Once the screws were undone the collars slid over the tubes and the whole frame came apart in four pieces. Inside each tube I was then able to roll up wads of Twenty Pound notes. I pushed each wad in place, using a wooden stick about three times the thickness of a pencil. I'd got the idea for this from watching the film Easy Rider on BBC2 last Saturday night. In the film they had hidden wads of money inside plastic tubes, which they hid in the fuel tank of a motorbike - ingenious! It took me the whole of Wednesday afternoon to roll up the money. When I'd filled up the four tubes there was two thousand five hundred and eighty pounds in total. I also ordered five hundred pounds in travellers cheques from four different Branches of the Midland Bank. And I also exchanged a thousand pounds equally in French Francs and Spanish Pesetas. There was still the majority money left over and it had to be stashed away again, back behind the shed. It had hardly made any difference to the size of the stash. Thursday morning the slabs were back in place with a scattering of leaves, covering up the recent disturbance. I hoped it would remain intact until I was back home again. If Mum or Dad were to find it I'm not sure how they would react, haul me off to the cop shop probably. Since Max's death everyone had been very kind to me. Madge and Joanie understood I needed time to myself. They were expecting me to leave the café one day soon anyway as they all knew I'd applied to join the RAF but still they told me not to make any rash decisions. My job at The Friary would be waiting for me if I wanted to come back at anytime. Even Edward offered me some helpful advise about continuing my education. 'You're a bright lad Byrney. You could do anything if you put your mind to it.' I told them all I was going to France, without giving away too many details. Mum and Dad on the other hand were shocked and disappointed that I'd not immediately accepted the offer from the RAF for an engineering apprenticeship and nine years service. I told them I needed to think about it. Nine years was a long time and I wasn't in the best frame of mind just now to make such an important decision. I didn't mention that they were putting pressure on me, but I felt it all the same. Mum and Dad almost fell out with each other over my decision, but Dad rallied round telling Mum I was sensible enough to make my own mind up. Then came the bombshell I was going abroad for a couple of weeks. If you're handing out bad news, might as well get it all out in the open at the same time. Mum didn't speak to me for the rest of the week until earlier this morning. "What was the point in having a passport if I wasn't going to use it?" I wished I'd phrased that a little bit better, but unfortunately, Mum was also having trouble getting used to the fact, I was now an adult. The only person who gave me a real hard time last week not surprisingly was Max's Mum.

I went to see her after my road trip and immediately after seeing Fionn. She wasn't surprised to see me. I knocked on the door and begged her to hear me out. I explained what had happened that day and what Max was like when I left her alone in the house. I told Max's Mum how guilty I felt about leaving her. If only I'd stayed with her, Max would still be alive. Max's Mum answered by saying "You don't know the half of it." God I hate this particular phrase. Whenever I hear it said to me it always makes me feel insignificant.

"What do you mean by that exactly? I've come here in good faith, I have no wish to fall out with you Mrs Reid."

Max's Mum looked like she might be thawing slightly as she opened the door wide enough for me to enter. "You'd better come in." She began by saying that no one could have prevented Max from taking her own life. "You see, it's not the first time she'd tried to commit suicide." I could feel my hand shaking so I put it behind my back out of view. "When Max was six years old she went through a very traumatic time. I'm not going to go into any detail with you, but needless to say she was out of school for quite a while. When she eventually went back she had problems settling in and eventually we relocated. About this time her father was drinking rather a lot and making both our lives very unpleasant. Max begged me to leave him. When nothing happened she drank half a bottle of spirits and took and overdose of pain killers. She was in hospital for over a week and in that time I'd managed to get a restraining order against my husband. Max was always haunted by her father. He was a terribly wicked person. I never blamed myself for the way he treated Max or for the way Max reacted to it. I've done my best to protect her. I even swore I'd never get married again. So you see it's not entirely your fault she's dead." There she goes, always a sting in her tail. I decided to show Max's Mum the suicide letter that Max had wrote to me, hoping she might get a better understanding of how deeply Max and me loved one another. She read it without saying a word or even showing the slightest emotion. When she'd finished, she folded it and handed it back to me.

"Since I got back from Canada I've not had the courage yet to enter Max's bedroom. You'd better go up and help yourself."

I got the impression that Max's Mum was only concerned with defending her reputation. I removed my shoes and climbed the stairs. The black and yellow hazard sign was still hanging outside Max's door. Looking round her brightly lit room, it was pure Max, exactly as I remembered it from the summer. I was half expecting Max to come waltzing back in at any minute, swinging her arms and teasing me with her extraordinary smile. I was aware that Max's Mum was downstairs, probably watching the clock too, so I quickly took Max's doll from the shelf. As I picked it up I could feel something beneath the dolls dress about the shape and size of a pack of cards. I stepped over Max's discarded clothes that littered the floor. At the bottom of her bed was the cropped t-shirt she'd been wearing that day we'd rode over to Cockerham sands. I picked it up, stuffed inside my jacket pocket, took one last look and closed the door behind me. I slid my shoes back on and went into the lounge holding up the doll for Max's Mum to see.

"Sorry I missed Max's funeral yesterday. I didn't feel comfortable about being there." I lied.

"No matter, it was only a small gathering, one or two of her friends and two from the café."

"Before I go, can I ask you what's going to happen to Max's ashes?"

Max's Mum looked at me smugly "Her ashes? There aren't any. I had her buried at St. Mary's."

"Buried! Max would have hated that. How could you?"

"I wanted Max near me, she was all I had left. Besides it's none of your business."

"Max was right about you, you are a selfish cow. You *never* loved her."

Max's Mum stood up in a rage. "Get out!" she screeched, grabbing my arm and began pushing me out of the room.

I brushed her off, "okay keep your hair on, I'm going." I hoped I'd never see her again. How could she be so callous? One day I would get even with her. If I'd had the time I would have dug Max up and set her in a burning boat, floating out to sea from Cockerham sands. Maybe I will one day.

Max's doll now sits on top of my wardrobe, out of reach of prying hands. I asked Mum to keep it safe and not let anyone touch it, especially our Anthony. The pack of cards hidden in the dolls dress was not a pack of cards at all. It was a diary from 1963. On the first page was the name Kate Reid. Was this Max's older sister? It would explain a lot, I thought. Was this Max's traumatic time? I stored the diary on my bookcase for later, one mystery at a time Byrney.

As it got near my train departure time, I was beginning to think I would be travelling alone after all. Then, walking down the steps from the overhead gantry I saw Fionn. She was wrapped up like a market stall at Christmas, woolly hat and scarf, gloves and wearing a red Parka with a furry collar. I had to laugh. I stood up and waved so that she could see where I was. When she was about three feet away, she leapt forward and landed with her arms around my neck. I'd never seen her as excited as this before. A railway guard, who'd been watching Fionn looked across at us, smiling away and said,

"That was really lovely. Seeing you two just now has made my day." We both looked at him and laughed.

"Blimey!" I said letting go of her "We're going to Paris, not the North Pole."

"It's my Mum," said Fionn "You know what she's like. Wanted to make sure I'd everything I might need."

"They have shops in France too you know." I joked. Then, on a more serious note, I asked, "Did you manage to speak to Henri Larouchamps in Nice?" I was hoping our plans were still on.

"Yes, he was lovely about it. Don't think he was expecting anyone to take up his offer so quickly, but he was really helpful. Mum had a word with him too. You know how Mums tend to worry? She probably thought he was running a brothel or something," she laughed

"Oh! You mean he isn't, that's a shame." Which earned me a slap on the shoulder from Fionn.

"Don't go spoiling it. He seemed quite enthusiastic about offering me a job."

I pulled a face at her

"Not that sort of job, you idiot."

It was going to be quite an adventure. Fionn was shaping up to be a great travel companion. That sounded like I was being unkind. We'd been friends a long time and hopefully that would ensure we stuck together, if things didn't go according to plan. I was really excited about my forthcoming adventure over the next few weeks too.

A scrambled voice came out over the Station public address system announcing the imminent arrival of the Inter-City Service to Euston Station. "That's us." Fionn began to peel off some of her woolly layers, stuffing them in the top of her red tartan rucksack. That should be easy to spot I thought. "Here let me give you a hand." and I held onto her Parka whilst she threw her rucksack back over her shoulders. The train was slowly screeching to a halt. Our friendly railway guard kindly opened the door for us with a smile and then moved further down the platform to the next carriage. Our carriage was almost empty so we stored our rucksacks in the cubby hole. I placed mine at the bottom then we went and sat at the first seat. I sat facing the door so that I could keep an eye on both our rucksacks.

"Are you really going to Spain?" asked Fionn

"Yer, eventually, or at least as far as The Pyrenees, but only after we get you settled in at the Hotel Les Moulins in Nice. No rush though, let's play it by ear."

"What did Madge and Joanie say when you told them you were leaving? Bet they're going to miss you?"

"First they told me what they'd said to you, about being welcome back anytime so they pretty much said the same thing to me too, apart from how all the cyclists would be fed up when they'd found out I've left."

I left Fionn to her thoughts as I stared out the window. My attention was drawn to an old pensioner carrying a small dog in a basket. The dog was doing it's best to escape. I was thinking about my own escape too. I thought if the Police were going to arrest me for the robbery, then this must be their final chance. I couldn't see a navy blue uniform, anywhere in insight. The guard blew his whistle and the last open doors were slammed tightly shut. At the last second, two more passengers entered our carriage, still holding their tickets. The two men barged their way through the inter-connecting carriage doors. The one at the back was a huge, mean looking guy with ginger hair. He glanced over at me for an instant. I hoped I wasn't sat in his seat, but they moved briskly past and settled down at the opposite end of the carriage. The train lurched forward with a little roar of the engine and crawled out of the Station and into the morning sunshine.

Fionn and I smiled at one another. I put my hands inside my jacket pockets and pulled out two cans of Colt 45.

"Fancy a beer, Fi?"

9 781915 889553